W9-AAB-308

HOW TO DISAPPEAR COMPLETELY and NEVER BE FOUND

HOW TO DISAPPEAR COMPLETELY and NEVER BE FOUND

Sara Nickerson

ILLUSTRATIONS BY SALLY WERN COMPORT

HARPERCOLLINS*PUBLISHERS*

This is a novel because Alix Reid said it should be.
And because of Stewart Stern, Geof Miller, and, of course, Alex Kuo.
It's a novel because I was given the perfect amount of time, space,
belief, and support. And for that I thank Matthew.

How to Disappear Completely and Never Be Found
Copyright © 2002 by Sara Nickerson
Illustrations © 2002 by Sally Wern Comport
All rights reserved. No part of this book may be used or reproduced in any manner
whatsoever without written permission except in the case of brief quotations
embodied in critical articles and reviews. Printed in the United States of America.
For information address HarperCollins Children's Books, a division of
HarperCollins Publishers, 1350 Avenue of the Americas, New York, NY 10019.
www.harperchildrens.com

Library of Congress Cataloging-in-Publication Data
Nickerson, Sara.
    How to disappear completely and never be found / by Sara Nickerson ;
illustrations by Sally Wern Comport.
        p.   cm.
    Summary: With a swimming medal, the key to a mansion, and a comic book
about a half-man/half-rat as her only clues, a twelve-year-old girl seeks the true
story of her father's mysterious death four eyars earlier near an island in the
Pacific Northwest.
    ISBN 0-06-029771-9 — ISBN 0-06-029772-7 (lib. bdg.)
    [1. Family life—Northwest, Pacific—Fiction.   2. Cartoons and comics—Fiction.
3. Recluses—Fiction.   4. Libraries—Fiction.   5. Northwest, Pacific—Fiction.
6. Mystery and detective stories.]   I. Comport, Sally Wern, ill.   II. Title.
PZ7.N55815 Ho   2002   2001039517
[Fic]—dc21   CIP
                                                                              AC

Typography by Hilary Zarycky
1   2   3   4   5   6   7   8   9   10
❖
First Edition

For Sara and Lindsey
Montana, 1993

CHAPTER 1

MOST STORIES START AT the beginning, but I really can't say I know where that is. Is it in a falling-down mansion on a small island in the Pacific Northwest, or in the navy blue pickup truck making its way to that mansion? Does it start on a sunny day this year, or a sunny day twenty years before? Is it with me, or with a young boy who, a long, long time ago, believed he was turning into a rat? I guess the only thing I do know is where it started for me—in that navy blue pickup heading toward a place I didn't know existed. A place that had already changed my life.

"I think we should move here. I think we should move here, Mom," said Sophie.

"We're not moving here."

"But if we moved here we could go swimming and buy a boat."

"We're not moving here," my mother said again. I reached over and turned the radio on, full blast.

"Margaret, I'm trying to talk," said Sophie, snapping it off.

"And I'm trying to think," I said.

"About what?"

"Give me five minutes of silence and maybe I'll tell you." Somehow that worked every time.

My little sister crossed her arms, sucked in a deep breath and held it. I glanced past her to my mother, busy chewing the pinky nail on her left hand all the way down to the skin.

"You should hold the wheel with two hands, Mom," I said. "Especially on the curves." Sophie let out a deep breath like she'd just surfaced from the bottom of the sea. "Not five minutes," I said to her, "not even close." Then, "Mom?"

Lizzie didn't answer, didn't even look my way, just took one last pinky nibble before gripping the steering wheel with both hands. The second I turned back to the window, though, she started in like I knew she would: ring finger, right hand. I watched her reflection in the window. Nibble, nibble, rip. I watched Sophie, too—her cheeks bulging like hard, round apples. This was my family.

I gave up. Would it really be so bad to crash and die on this remote island road? For all I cared at that moment, my mother could steer with her feet.

"It's been five minutes," Sophie announced loudly. I looked at my watch. It hadn't even been two.

"So?" I said. Outside, white-topped waves flung themselves against a rocky beach. I opened the window just enough to let fresh air swirl into the truck. It was the middle of March, only one week away from the first day of spring, and the air smelled like damp earth and flowers.

"So you have to tell me. What were you thinking?"

I rolled the window up, rolled it down again, hummed a little tune, then glanced sideways at my mother. She'd run out of fingernails and had started to bite the skin off her bottom lip. "I was just wondering why the big mystery," I said.

Sophie glanced over at our mother. "It's not a total mystery," she said. "We know some things." My sister and I are like a teeter-totter: When I am at my lowest low, she is up, up, up.

"No," I said, "we don't." But even as I said it, I knew Sophie was right—we did know some things. "We can assume that we own something on this island," I said, "and that we're going to sell it. But, hmmm. What could that be? I don't remember ever being on this island before. Do you, Sophie?"

Sophie shook her head, her eyes still fixed on Lizzie. I sighed and turned back to the window. The answer wouldn't come from our mother, I knew that much. But it would come in time. There was a sign in the back of the truck that said For Sale by Owner. The answer would come in time. It had to.

Already I think I need to back up, to the same day, but a few hours earlier. I was in the kitchen, washing the dishes that had stacked up during the week. Sophie was sitting on the counter next to me, slurping milk from a bowl. From the living room came the sound of a wild animal and the smell of smoke. I glanced at my little sister, wondering if she was thinking the same thing I was. See, our mother watches nature programs every weekend, but she only smokes when something is wrong.

I heard the sofa creak, then footsteps across the living room carpet. A moment later Lizzie stood in the kitchen, leaned against the far counter and squinted at us through a cloud of thick, gray smoke. She tapped her fingers against the side of her ceramic coffee mug and started to hum some sort of cross between "Happy Birthday to You" and "The Itsy-Bitsy Spider" until I couldn't take it anymore.

"It's Sunday, Mom. Why are you wearing lipstick?" Her mouth was smeared chalky red, slapped on in a hurry and without a mirror. Her shoulder-length hair was pulled back in a tight but messy ponytail, like she'd forgotten to brush it first.

Lizzie didn't answer me. She took a last swig of coffee, then crushed her cigarette in the bottom of the cup, making a little fizzy sound. Like magic, another cigarette appeared between the V of her fingers. She lit it quickly, took in a deep breath and somehow managed to say, "Get your shoes," without letting it out. I stared at her, waiting for the exhalation. *One thousand one, one thousand two.* "Shoes and jackets," she breathed out finally. Smoke and words swirled around the kitchen while, from the living room, an angry lion roared.

Sophie had hopped off the counter and raced down the hallway at the first mention of shoes. From the small bedroom we shared she called out excitedly, "Margaret, do you want me to get yours, too?"

"No," I called back. I continued to rinse the soap off the dishes, taking too much time with each one.

"You can do those later," said Lizzie, still tapping, still humming, still blowing smoke.

"It's Sunday, Mom," I said again. "Where are we going?"

"Just get your shoes," was all she said.

Ten minutes later, when we were all three squeezed in the front of the pickup, Lizzie lit up her fourth cigarette of the morning and started the engine.

"Where are we going, Mom? Going, Mom?" Sophie jumped up and down in perfect time to each word. *Going, going, going, Mom.*

Of course I knew why she was excited. If you look up "predictable" in the dictionary, it tells you to spend a weekend at our house. First there's Saturday. Saturdays are what Sophie calls Family Fun Day, but that's not what I would call them. I would call them Bare Minimum for Survival Day, and here's how they go. At about three o'clock, after Lizzie's had both her morning and afternoon nap, we gather up our dirty clothes from the week, toss them in the back of the truck and head to the Laundromat. The first thing we do there is sort by color—whites with whites, darks with darks, and mediums with mediums. I fought this at first, wanting to keep all my clothes in one machine so they wouldn't mix with Sophie's, but after Lizzie actually let me try it and everything turned pinkish-gray, I am now a firm believer in sorting. Whites, darks, mediums, and delicates.

"What's delicates?" Sophie once asked, and when Lizzie answered, "Pretty nightgowns and things," Sophie demanded that her Tigger pajamas go into that pile. Even though Lizzie stood firm and told her they didn't, every week Sophie yells, "Delicates!" and throws her Tigger pajamas around the Laundromat, just for fun.

When the machines are sudsing and grinding, I settle down with my *National Geographic* magazine while Sophie carefully arranges completed chunks of THE HARDEST JIGSAW EVER MADE onto the laundry sorting table. This is the puzzle that, if she ever manages to complete, will award her with a framed certificate; *plus* she'll have her name added to a list of all the other weirdos in the world who have also managed to put it together. I think there are five.

Lizzie always takes a paperback from her bag, places it on her lap and immediately falls asleep. I once asked her why she even bothered bringing a book, but she just looked at me like she had no idea what I was talking about.

After the machines have finished their rinse cycle, I help Sophie put away her puzzle. This usually takes the exact length of the spin cycle. Then we toss the wet clothes into the dryers, shake Lizzie awake and the three of us walk a block and a half to the grocery store. At the store Lizzie pushes the shopping cart while Sophie and I pick out the food.

Now, I know this might sound like fun, but it's really not. Not even for Sophie. First we stop at the bakery where, every week, we buy the same two loaves of bread—one white and one wheat. I once made a mistake and picked up sourdough, so now I'm extra careful about reading labels.

After the bakery we move to the cereal aisle. Since we can pick anything we want, this is the most interesting part of the trip. Every week Sophie makes a point of choosing a different cereal for herself. She gets very serious and walks up and down the aisle several times, studying each box carefully. When she finds the prize or cartoon or smiling face on the front of the box that gives her a special "this cereal will make your life better" signal, she pulls it from the shelf gently and carries it the rest of the shopping trip, clutched to her chest like a beloved doll.

I, on the other hand, have learned to stick with cornflakes. Even though there's never a crossword printed on the box or a toy surprise inside, I know I can depend on a bowl of cornflakes. I guess that's the difference between being seven and being twelve.

The rest of the shopping trip is like clockwork. Milk, bananas, chips, peanut butter and jelly, and, the staple of our lives, frozen foods. There's no browsing in this section—we know exactly what we need for the week. Six frozen pizzas (three cheese, three pepperoni), two bags of Tater Tots, and six microwave Bean-O Burritos. Done. Lizzie once picked up a bag of frozen peas and mumbled something about "more green things," but they've been sitting frozen for nearly a year now. Every time I open the freezer door and see their blank round heads staring back at me, I feel a little sad. *One more thing missing from your life*, they seem to say.

With the shopping cart fully loaded, we zip through our favorite checkout line (number four—it has the best magazine rack) and get back to the Laundromat, usually just in time for the clothes to be making their final tumble in the dryer. We throw everything—groceries, clothes, books, THE HARDEST JIGSAW EVER MADE—into the back of the truck and head for home. Then, while Mom curls up on the couch, Sophie and I unload the groceries and put away the clothes. The "fun" part of Family Fun Day is over.

Then comes Sunday, or what Lizzie likes to call Family Unwind Days. For her this means an entire morning and afternoon spent on the couch, drifting in and out of sleep while gruesome nature programs fill our house with sights and sounds of the wild. ("It's the only thing on TV worth watching," she'll say as a sleek cheetah rips apart yet another spindly gazelle.)

For Sophie, Family Unwind Day means spreading

out on the living room floor with—what else?—THE HARDEST JIGSAW EVER MADE. Only when she finishes it will she know what it's supposed to be. I guess that's what keeps people hooked, or something.

On Sundays I wash all the cups, bowls, and spoons that have stacked up during the week. Then I fold and put away my clean laundry from the day before. Then I rearrange the frozen food in the freezer and move the lone refrigerator magnet (a pink hippo saying "Feed Me"—a Mother's Day gift from Sophie two years ago) from one side of the refrigerator to the other. Sometimes I search the apartment for cracks or openings that an army of insects or a swarm of killer bees could use to find their way into our home.

And that's about it. We heat up a pizza or burrito, sometimes both, get to bed by nine because it's a school night, and five days later start the whole weekend thing over again. That's why this particular Family Unwind Day seemed so very exciting, so very strange.

When Sophie saw the sign pointing to the ferry terminal, she bounced so high her head hit the ceiling of the truck. "We're going on a ferry, we're going on a ferry," she shouted as Lizzie pulled up to the ticket booth.

Even though we live in a waterfront town and ferry boats are nearly as common as transit buses, still, there's something exciting about riding one. No matter what the weather is like, I always stand out on deck to study the tiny islands that seem to have fallen straight from the sky. I like to imagine hiding out on one, surviving on handfuls of wild huckleberries and fresh oysters straight from the shell. You could probably live on one of those unnamed islands for years and no one but maybe a sharp-eyed ferry captain would ever suspect.

I couldn't remember the last time we'd been on a ferry; I couldn't even remember the last time we'd left the apartment on a Sunday. So as I stood out on the deck, I had a strange feeling. I said the words to myself, then lifted my face and whispered them into the sharp wind.

"What?" Sophie was at my elbow, tugging on my sleeve. She'd been huddled next to me the whole time and I hadn't even noticed. "What did you say, Margaret?"

"Nothing," I said back to her. But to myself and the wind-tossed seagulls I said it again. *After today, nothing will ever be the same.*

The ferry worker waved her flag and Lizzie started the engine. Once again, we were all three squeezed in the front of the truck. My cheeks tingled from the windy ferry ride and my usually straight hair was a tangled mess around my face.

My mother cracked the truck window just enough to flick out the long, fragile ash of her cigarette, then she put the truck in gear and followed the small line of cars off the boat and up to the main road. When she reached the first intersection, she stopped. Looked left, then right. Switched her cigarette from one hand to the other, then began to nibble the nail on that pinky.

"Mom," Sophie asked, "have I ever been on this island before?"

Lizzie shook her head.

"Have *I* ever been here, Mom?" I asked. I felt like we were playing some sort of mystery game, but no one knew the rules.

My mother didn't answer, didn't nod or shake, just switched her cigarette back to the other hand again and turned left.

"Town," said Sophie, reading the sign. "The arrow pointed this way to town."

"If I remember right," Lizzie mumbled to herself, "there was a hardware store right around here."

So she, at least, had been here before. *Clue number one.*

Lizzie drove slowly through town, which was basically one long street flanked by a funny assortment of shops and businesses. There was a touristy shop with a window full of ceramic seagulls and hula girls made out of small, pink shells. There was a side-by-side barber shop–beauty parlor called His and Her Hair. A tavern with windows so dark I couldn't see inside, a post office and a drugstore and a coffee house and a lemon-yellow cottage with a sign that said LIBRARY.

"There it is," she said, pulling in front of a gray-shingled hardware shop with a faded U-FIX-IT sign.

"You didn't use your turn signal," I said.

My mother pulled on the emergency brake and acted like she hadn't heard. "Wait here," she said, opening the door and climbing out. "And don't let anyone steal you."

I watched her walk away from the truck—faded jeans, oversized sweater, and wispy brown hair that was already starting to slip from its ponytail—something about her seeming more overgrown sister than mother. I pictured her in the hardware store, wandering up and down every aisle, maybe even two or three times before finally finding what she was looking for. My mom lives in a world of her own. She doesn't know that people with the "Ask Me, I Know" buttons are there to help her.

"Why do you think we're here, Margaret?"

I shrugged like I didn't care.

"I wonder if it has something to do with Dad." Sophie surprised me sometimes. Even though she was just a baby when our father died, she seemed to understand the number one rule of our house: Don't talk about Dad in front of Mom.

I looked in the side-view mirror and pushed the tangled mess of hair back from my face. "Do you think I look more like her or him?" I asked.

"You know I don't remember what he looked like."

"You've seen pictures."

"Well, your eyes are like Mom's. Sort of like muddy water."

"Thanks."

"No, I mean in a good way. Like the ocean when it mixes with sand. Sort of blue and gray and brown."

Sophie's eyes were just one color—deep, rich brown, like a small, wild, woodsy creature. I turned back to the window, leaned my head against its cold, hard surface and closed my muddy-water eyes. *My father stands in front of me wearing a white T-shirt. He is laughing.* "That was real," I whispered, believing that if I could just take different bits of memory and line them all up, maybe I'd have a complete picture of him. I thought of Sophie's puzzle. My family was the genuine HARDEST JIGSAW EVER MADE.

"Why do you care, anyway? Who cares if you look more like Mom or Dad?" Sophie poked me in the arm. She gets nervous when I close my eyes during the day.

I kept my eyes closed and shrugged. Inherited traits—they were something I'd been thinking a lot about lately. Why did some bees make honey and others join a swarm that traveled the world on a killing spree? What made one puppy a tail-wagging family pet and another a vicious guard dog? Was there something I got from my father's side of the family that I didn't know about? That jigsaw of mine had a big hole, right smack in the middle. Sophie couldn't understand it now, but I knew someday she would.

"Was Dad crazy?"

I sat straight up and opened my eyes. "Sophie! Why would you ask that?"

"I don't know. Because of when Mom said you take after Dad's crazy side of the family."

"When did she say that?"

"You know. Right before she sent you to the uniform school."

A thud in the back of the truck kept Sophie from saying anything more. She turned to see what had made the noise, and then she started to bounce. "Margaret, Look! It's a sign."

I glanced over my shoulder, trying to pretend I really didn't care, but even I couldn't hide my surprise. *Okay, clue number two.*

Lizzie stood next to the truck, a fresh cigarette hanging from her fading lips. She glared at us a moment before opening the driver's-side door and sliding inside.

"What?" I said. "We didn't do anything."

"What's it mean, Mom? What's it mean?" Sophie looked from the sign, to me, to Lizzie, then back to the sign. "What's it mean, Mom? What's it mean?"

Lizzie started the engine and pretended to concentrate, a trick parents do when they don't want to answer a question. We drove back through town and made a couple of turns. Passed a dentist's office and a chiropractor, a video store and a brick newspaper building called the Weekly Islander. Five minutes later, though, it felt as though we were the only three people left in the world.

"Waterfront Road," said Sophie, reading the street sign. Then in a hushed voice she added, "It's like a giant cave of trees."

And it was. Flanked by hulking, moss-covered evergreens, Waterfront Road cut a dark, twisted path through the forest. "It feels like it's night now, doesn't it, Margaret?"

I nodded. Then shivered. I've always thought of trees as friendly spirits—you know, shade, shelter, photosynthesis—but these trees were not friendly at all. These trees seemed to resent the intrusion of the heavy concrete slab of road—and anyone who dared use it. "I don't get why it's called Waterfront Road," I said. "Shouldn't there be water?"

"Just wait," Lizzie answered, surprising me. Until that moment I hadn't thought she'd been listening to us at all.

As Lizzie drove too fast around a sharp, twisty corner, Sophie reached out and clutched my elbow. I stared out the window at the edge of the road. "You're too close on this side, Mom," I said.

"My friend at school—her dad drove into a deer once," Sophie added quickly. "He was going too fast and couldn't stop. He killed the deer and broke both his arms and one leg. But he couldn't even use crutches because of his arms."

Lizzie bit down on her knuckle as she took the

sharpest turn of all. I felt Sophie's other palm make a sweaty imprint on my forearm.

"Okay," Lizzie mumbled, shifting gears, "we can all relax now." In one instant the cave of somber trees and clinging moss had opened up to something different, something bright and beautiful. It was as though the forest had chewed us up and then, instead of swallowing, had decided to spit us out into a dizzying world of sunshine and clouds and water—the biggest, most pure blue stretch of water I had ever seen.

"Wow," said Sophie. "I think we should move here."

"We're not moving here."

"But if we moved here we could go swimming and buy a boat."

I reached over and turned the radio on, full blast. Which is, I guess, where I first started this story—with Lizzie eating her fingers, Sophie holding her breath, and me, staring out the window, trying to make sense of a For Sale by Owner sign that was sliding around the back of our pickup.

CHAPTER 2

BOYD LOOKED OUT HIS bedroom window. Something didn't seem right, but he couldn't say what exactly, or even why he felt it. Surrounded by overgrown weeds and bushes, the mansion next door stood as it always had—three stories of cracked and peeling paint, warped wood, a sagging porch. Some windows were boarded up with two-by-fours, but most of them had been broken, leaving sharp pieces of jagged glass to glitter dangerously in the bright spring sun. Only the large windows on the second floor and the attic were still intact, and Boyd stared at them a moment longer. Then, when he was sure nothing was out of place, he turned away from the window and back to his pile of comics on the bed.

Thwack!

Boyd rolled to the floor and held his breath. He waited several moments, then lifted his head cautiously. From outside his window came the sounds of rustling bushes, muffled laughter, then another *thwack!*

"Oh, no," he moaned to himself when he realized what was happening. It was the Threes again.

Very slowly and keeping his head low, he crawled to the window just as another rock flew across the sky and slammed against the side of the mansion. More laughter, louder this time, then another rock hit. And then another.

Boyd knew the Threes from school—three boys who stepped on the backs of his shoes and played keep-away with his comics. Busting windows on the old mansion was just another one of their pastimes. And although Boyd would have been very happy to never have to face any of them again, he shuddered to think about what could happen if they got caught.

Returning to his stack of comic books, Boyd searched until he found the one he was looking for—the one titled, *RATT VOLUME 89: WHAT HAPPENED WHEN THEY GOT CAUGHT*. On the cover was a perfect, hand-drawn replica of the mansion.

Boyd glanced out the window again. The boys, obviously feeling braver now, had ventured from their shadowy cover. On hands and knees and looking like soldiers from an old World War II movie, they inched their way toward the front steps of the mansion. Even with the sunlight streaming into his bedroom, Boyd suddenly felt cold. It looked like—but it couldn't be! Were the Threes actually planning to break in?

He closed his eyes, waiting for the screams that would come the minute the boys made it past the front porch. But instead he heard something completely different; instead he heard *cr—unch*. He opened his eyes to a navy blue pickup turning into the mansion's old gravel drive.

Boyd had never seen any sort of vehicle pull into

the drive before. He watched the Threes scatter like crabs, back to the safety of the bushes where their bikes were stashed. He watched the lady park the truck. He watched the two girls next to her—the little one bouncing up and down, the bigger one scowling at the mansion. Boyd watched and waited.

CHAPTER 3

"*I THINK WE SHOULD* move here, Mom," said Sophie, pawing at me to get to the door.

"I heard you the first time, Sophie," Lizzie answered. "You don't have to say it ever again." She shoved her hand in the crack of the seat, searching for her lighter.

I looked up at the huge old house. *For Sale by Owner?*

"This place is like a palace," said Sophie, still pushing for the door. "If we lived here we'd have the sea for a backyard." When I didn't budge, she grunted like a little pig.

"Mom, is this place ours?" I asked. We'd passed a few lonely houses along the road, but I never thought we'd be pulling into the driveway of one—and especially one like this. Sophie was right—it was like a palace. But a palace that was under a dark spell. Towering bushes and massive blackberry hedges kept it pretty much hidden from the road, and even its backdrop of sparkling blue water somehow seemed colder than the water lapping up against the rest of the beach. Only one thing came close to breaking the spell, and that was the house next door—as completely ordinary as the mansion was strange. Beige and white with a station wagon in the driveway, it looked like it was plucked straight from some modern, sprawling housing development. And even though it sat close to the mansion, there was something about its tidy lawn and curtained windows that seemed to say, "Strange old house next door? What strange old house?"

I turned back to the mansion. "Mom," I said again, "is this place really—"

"Mom! Tell Margaret to move," Sophie interrupted. "I can't *breathe!*"

Still fishing for her lighter, Lizzie ignored us both. She'd already come up with a dime and two quarters, a silver hoop earring, and a dried bean. "Ah-ha," she said when she finally pulled out the lighter. She settled back and opened her door, making way for Sophie to scramble across her lap. I watched my sister tumble to the ground, jump up, and run straight for the yard where she raced around wildly, waving her arms at the gnarled bushes and huge, prickly hedges.

Lizzie lit her cigarette. She sucked in a deep, long breath. "Take that sign and stick it in the middle of the yard, would you?" she said. When she spoke, smoke shot out of her nostrils. "But first take this marker and write our phone number near the bottom."

I glanced at the sign in the back of the truck, then at the thick, permanent-ink marker that she had pulled out from the bottom of her purse. "So why is it ours, Mom?"

"Just do it, please."

"But Lizzie—"

"Please, Margaret. And don't call me Lizzie. I'm your mother." She tossed the pen my way and leaned her head back, forcing out two more streams of gray nostril smoke.

I grabbed the pen and, just because I felt like it, slammed the truck door so hard the windows shook. Lizzie didn't even seem to notice. "You look like a dragon!" I shouted as I grabbed the sign from the back of the truck and scribbled our phone number in the empty space near the bottom.

Lizzie rolled down her window. "Somewhere in the middle of the yard," she called out sleepily.

I stomped into the yard, kicking at weeds and thistles.

"What are you doing, Margaret?" Sophie ran up to me all red and sweaty and out of breath. Little pig girl, I wanted to say.

"None of your business," I said.

"If it's your business, it's my—"

"Shut up, Sophie. Just for one minute. Then I'll tell you." I lifted the sign high over my head. I felt like a monster, a warrior, a dragon slayer. I aimed the pointed end and stabbed it to the ground. It bounced right back without even making a dent. "Damn!" I said.

"I'm telling," said Sophie.

I dropped the sign and examined my stinging hands for splinters. Lizzie, deciding to play mom for a moment, called out in a concerned voice, "What's the matter, honey?"

"Margaret said a bad word."

"What's the matter, Margaret?" Lizzie asked again.

"The ground is too hard," I said. "It won't go in."

"She said 'damn.' Does For Sale by Owner mean this is ours?"

"The ground is really too hard?" Lizzie opened the door and stepped out of the truck.

"Yes, Mom. It is really too hard." I pulled a long, sharp splinter out of my hand.

Sophie picked up the sign, held it high above her head and ran around the yard yelling, "Our house, our house, our house, our house."

"Sophie!" Lizzie called. "Give me that!" She walked across the yard nervously, like it might be full of quicksand or rattlesnakes. Land mines. She snatched the sign away from Sophie, then stood in the middle of the yard like she wasn't quite sure what to do next.

"Why is it ours, Mom?" I asked.

Lizzie shaded her eyes from the sun and glanced around, as if seeing the place for the first time. I followed her gaze, from the crumbling shingles on the side of the house to a long sloping field that led down to the rocky beach, about two hundred yards behind it. The field was covered with golden beach grasses and purple and yellow wildflowers; the breeze coming up from the water was salty and clean. "It's almost pretty, isn't it?" Lizzie said softly. Then, before I could answer she added, "Watch your sister. Don't let her go down to the water. I'll go look for something to loosen the ground. A hoe or something." She dropped the sign in the middle of the yard and made her way to the side of the house, still stepping carefully. I watched her disappear around the corner, holding her arms to her chest like she was freezing cold, even under a sun so bright.

"Mom said not to go up there."

I was standing at the foot of the steps, wondering how much time I had before Lizzie returned with the shovel or hoe. Sophie was right behind me, breathing hard. "No she didn't," I said. "She said for you not to go down by the water."

I don't know if it was the salty breeze or the fact that we were standing in the shadow of the house, but at that very moment, something made me shiver. I looked at Sophie's skinny arms—she had goose bumps, too.

"Are you going in?" Sophie whispered.

"No," I lied. "Go back and play in the yard."

Sophie turned and trotted back to the hedges, humming. I took a deep breath. This was my chance.

Creak. The front steps were old and rotting. Fat, shiny insects, not used to being disturbed, poured out of invisible cracks in the wood. They raced around nervously—up and down and across the tops of my shoes.

All I wanted was to look through a slit in the boarded-up window, or maybe even push open the front door. All I wanted was to get a glimpse at what was inside this house For Sale by Owner.

Creak. On the third step I got the feeling that something wasn't quite right. Creak. On the fourth step I realized what: It was way too quiet.

"Sophie!" I jumped off the steps and looked around the yard. "Sophie!" The hedges stood tall and secretive and smug. *See what happens?* they seemed to say.

"Sophie!" I called again, aiming for the perfect balance between loud enough and not too loud. If Mom heard me calling for my lost sister, I'd be dead.

I ran around to the side of the house and down toward the water, stumbling through the waist-high beach grasses, calling out her name.

And then I stopped. The edge of the field was that abrupt—like the thin blue line that marks a margin on a piece of paper. Like the end of the world before it was round.

Having lived all my life in a waterfront town, I'd seen plenty of beaches, but never one as wild and untouched as this. Bright orange starfish squeezed their arms around craggy oyster shells while shiny black mussels lay under thick blankets of slimy green seaweed; jagged rocks stood guard over foamy tide pools, so brimming with sea life they looked like some sort of dangerous and exotic soup. The only sign of civilization was a small, wooden dock that jutted out over the water.

THE PARK RIDGE PUBLIC LIBRARY

The dock was old and rickety; tied to its end was a canoe—a blue canoe, painted so that on a sunny day, it blended almost perfectly with the water. It was so perfect, in fact, that I might have missed it if not for the small girl at the end of the dock, leaning out over the water and tugging on the rope that kept the canoe from floating out to sea. "Sophie!"

Relieved, I made my way across the beach, careful not to disturb the starfish and mussels and tide-pool soup. "Mom told you not to go down here." But Sophie didn't even glance my way.

I stepped up onto the dock and walked the length of it, liking how my steps sounded slightly hollow—both a part of me and a part of something else. Even though it was weathered and worn, the dock felt good and sturdy under my feet, the way wood sometimes does.

I knelt down next to my sister, who was playing tug-of-war with the tide and the waves. "Help me get it, Margaret," she said, her eyes never leaving the canoe. "Maybe we can take it home."

Without thinking, I reached out and grabbed the rope on either side of her small, clenched hands. With a tug, the canoe came forward, its long nose gently nudging the end of the dock. As I held it in place, Sophie tenderly stroked the smooth, painted wood. "Hello," she whispered, like she was trying to win over some soft, shy creature. Then to me she said, "Let's get in."

"There isn't a paddle."

"Just to sit. We'll keep it tied to the dock. Just to sit and rock with the waves."

I glanced back at the house, wondering how long we had before Lizzie came looking for us. And that's when I saw it, a quick flicker of movement in one of the upstairs windows. Like someone had just passed by. Like someone had been watching.

"Sophie, look," I said. "I think Mom's in the house." But even as I said it, Lizzie's voice came shooting across the field—a silver bullet, a blazing cannonball, a flaming arrow.

"Uh-oh," said Sophie.

"Margaret! Sophie! Get away from that water!"

"Sophie," I said with a sigh, "you get me in the biggest trouble."

Sophie started to giggle just as Lizzie busted through the weeds and tripped up onto the rocky beach. "What's so funny?" she demanded. Tiny white crabs scurried for cover as she marched toward us. When she stepped onto the dock, the wood creaked an angry protest, making Sophie laugh even more.

Lizzie reached us in three big strides. *Creak, creak, creak.* She leaned down and grabbed Sophie by the elbows. "What's so funny, Missy? You think this is funny?" Pulling Sophie to her feet, Lizzie half pushed, half carried her to shore. "Come on, Margaret," she called back over her shoulder. "And watch your step."

I let go of the rope and slowly stood up. The pretty

blue canoe bobbed its pointed nose at me. "Were you in the house just now, Mom?" But Lizzie was already halfway up the field.

I stepped off the dock and zigzagged my way across the beach, keeping my eyes on that one upstairs window. Maybe I'd just seen a reflection in the glass, I told myself. The sun off the water, or a bird or a cloud. But even as I thought it, I shivered. For the second time in that bright sunshine, I shivered. Something about the place wasn't right. I could feel it. And I knew my mom could feel it, too.

By the time I'd caught up with them, Sophie (long over the giggles) was being held prisoner inside the truck, while Prison Warden Lizzie stomped around in an angry cloud of dust and smoke. When she saw me, she yanked the cigarette from her mouth long enough to remind me that people drown in their own bathtubs; they drown in mud puddles, while drinking out of water faucets and, sometimes even, from talking too much during heavy rains. Then she told me to go to the back of the house and retrieve the shovel she'd dropped when she heard us down by the water. "And come right back," she shouted after me, "there's rusty nails everywhere!"

I spotted the shovel right away, but wanted to explore a little before taking it back to the truck. Attached to the back of the house was one of those enclosed porches, the kind with walls and a ceiling and a door of its own. Since the door was open just a crack (probably where Lizzie had found the shovel), I decided to take a peek. Just one look inside this strange house—that was all I wanted.

Do you know that feeling of doing something and at the same time of watching yourself do it? It's like watching a movie but you *are* the movie. And you're watching yourself talk and walk, but the whole time you're holding your breath and thinking, *What is she going to do next?* Well, that was me, watching the movie of me: I climbed the steps; I put my hand on the door. My heart was thumping *stop, stop, stop* on the inside of my chest, but I watched myself push the door open. I watched myself step inside.

The porch felt like a place long forgotten, like the air inside hadn't moved in years. It was packed floor to ceiling with—well, things. Things you think about and things you don't. Things that make up the world. There were wooden pickle barrels and rusted gates and tools to fix a car and tools to fix a tooth and tools to build a house. There were bicycle horns and balls of string and at least a dozen different mannequin hands, all with the same chipped red polish; there were stubs of candles and old-fashioned ruffled dresses and doll heads with missing hair and baby bottles and at least three, maybe four, motorcycle helmets. Cans of food without the labels and garbage sacks full of toilet paper rolls. I could have stayed on that porch for days, digging through piles of twenty-year-old *National Geographic*s and crinkly yellowed newspapers with funny-looking ads. But I knew I didn't have days and the thing I most wanted was a peek inside the house. Just a peek.

I took a step forward, then another and another. This wasn't so easy, since I had to move rusty fishing poles and boxes of Christmas tree ornaments before each new step. I tripped over a crate full of ency-clopedias and felt something collapse with a crack, leaving me flat on my face, chewing on dust and spiderwebs. I shifted gingerly to my side and looked down at the box I'd crashed through—an old wooden crate with a makeshift lid. And that's when I saw it.

Sometimes a thing can be so familiar—as familiar as your own face—but because you weren't expecting to see it, you don't recognize it right away. It happened to me only one other time, on the elevator in the apartment building where we live. I'd left school early and had gone home, knowing that no one else would be there. Even though our apartment building is only three stories high and we're on the second floor, I decided to take the elevator, just for fun. When it reached our floor, the door opened and a girl stood in front of me. I stared at her and she stared at me, then suddenly, at the exact same moment we realized we were sisters. Sophie had come home because she'd forgotten her lunch. "I didn't know who you were for a second," she said, giggling. I laughed, too. I can't now remember what her face looked like as a stranger, but I know it looked different than it looks as a sister.

Anyway, that's what happened when I realized what I was looking at—a small package tucked in the corner of the crate. A small package addressed to Elizabeth Clairmont. Elizabeth Clairmont. The name was so familiar—I knew I knew it from somewhere. And then it hit me like Sophie's face at the elevator. Of course I knew the name. I was Clairmont, too. And Elizabeth—that was long for Lizzie, my mother. And of course the writing looked familiar: "Return to Sender" was scribbled in her own hasty hand.

Someone had sent this to my mother.

And she had sent it back.

I picked it up, brushed off the dust and turned it over in my hand. The package had never even been opened. I checked the postmark—four years old.

Someone had sent this to my mother.

And she had sent it back.

From far off came the sound of a truck horn. I heard it like I was underwater or in the very middle of some strange and puzzling dream. *Come back*, the horn cried, *come back.*

I watched the movie of me stuff the package down the back of my jeans and pull my sweatshirt low to cover it. I watched myself stumble off the porch and down the stairs and into the weeds.

I knew I couldn't let Lizzie see what I'd found. She would hide it away and never say another word about it. The horn blasted again and I started to run. I couldn't let Sophie see it, either. She would tell Lizzie.

H-O-N-K. I ran around the side of the house and back toward my mother and sister and the honking truck. I ran and felt the package rub against my back and it felt strange and good and sort of scary, too. I ran fast because I had a feeling in my stomach that was making me run fast. I had the feeling in my stomach, but I couldn't let my head think what it meant, not yet anyway. *Four years ago, four years.* I was almost to the truck when I remembered the shovel.

CHAPTER 4

THE BLAST OF THE horn startled Boyd out of his Sunday afternoon daydream. Earlier he'd been at the window watching them—the lady pacing along the side of the truck while the girl, the little one, turned somersaults in the front seat. But after several minutes of nothing new, Boyd had returned to his bed and the stack of waiting comics.

H-O-N-K. The second blast brought him racing back to the window. The lady was still pacing, but now the little girl was at the steering wheel with her hand poised over the horn. *H-O-N-K*.

The other girl came running around the side of the house, her cheeks flushed and hair flying. In her hands was an old, rusted shovel that she carried like a prized trophy. Boyd watched as the lady met the girl in the middle of the yard, took the shovel and began to hack at the tough, crusted ground. He watched her stick a sign in the middle of the yard and pile dirt around its base.

A sign? In the yard? Boyd ducked away from the window. A moment later he heard the truck engine rumble to life, then the crunch of wheels on the gravel drive. When he looked back out, they were gone.

He let out a sigh of relief. Maybe everything was fine. Maybe everything would be okay. After all, the lady and the girls had been on the front porch and at the back of the house and even down by the water and none of them had gotten hurt. Boyd shuddered as he thought about what could have happened. No, no one had gotten hurt. *Yet.*

CHAPTER 5

"*THERE WAS A HOUSE*, a beautiful house, they could have swimmed all day." Once again, Sophie was squished up next to me, singing just loud enough for Lizzie to hear, but not so loud that she'd tell her to stop.

"Stop," I said finally.

Sophie ignored me. "There was a house, a beautiful house—"

I turned my body sideways and pressed my face against the cold glass of the window. As we pulled into the ferry terminal and lined up with the other cars waiting to board, Lizzie reached for her pack of cigarettes.

My mother gets nervous about a lot of things, but because of the way my dad died, water is the worst—which is why she was so angry to find us out on the dock. And why Sophie's never had a swimming lesson. Even sitting on a ferry makes my mother's blood pressure rise. I think she was glad Sophie had misbehaved, because she now had an excuse to punish her (and me!) by making us sit in the truck the entire ferry ride home. No deck, no seagulls, no tiny islands.

Sophie had pouted at first, then decided to see how many times she could turn around in her seat, like a puppy chasing its tail. But by then I almost didn't notice since I had other things, more important things, to think about. Like the sign we'd planted in the yard of a strange old house and a shiny blue canoe bobbing on the water. Like the bulky piece of a puzzle, four years old and addressed to my mother, jabbing me in my back.

CHAPTER 6

FROM HIS BEDROOM BOYD could hear his mother and father in the kitchen, clattering pots and pans. His parents had recently switched to a macrobiotic diet, which meant several different bowls of green food and maybe one or two bowls of brown. The only thing on the table that was not green or brown was Boyd's foamy white glass of milk—and lately there'd been talk of substituting that with something made of beans. ("Soymilk, Boyd," his father had said. "You can't even tell the difference.") In fact, all dinnertime conversation was now about food, which made Boyd wonder if it was being a grown-up or eating a macro- biotic diet that made a person really boring.

"Boyd! Dinner!" his father called from the dining room.

"Tell him to wash his hands," he heard his mother add.

"Wash your hands, son!"

Boyd marked the page in his comic book and took one last look out the window. *It wouldn't be a full moon for a few days*, he thought with relief. Full moons were the worst.

"Pass the rice, please."

Boyd put down his chopsticks (the silverware had

also disappeared with the meatloaf and cheesy casseroles) and passed the green bowl of brown to his mother.

"So," said his father with a nod, "I think adding seaweed to the rice was a great idea."

"I agree," said his mother. "Boyd?"

Boyd finished his milk in one gulp and held up his empty glass. "Can I get another?"

His parents exchanged glances. "One more," said his father finally. "Then that's it for today."

Boyd headed to the kitchen, thankful that the next day was Monday. Not that he loved school or anything, but he could usually save enough change to buy a milkshake or a burger at the local drugstore in town. Boyd survived the weekends by what he managed to scrape up during the week. "Like a rat," he said softly as he filled his glass with milk. The thought made him smile.

Dishes washed, garbage emptied, homework finished, good-nights said, and Boyd was back in his bedroom, snuggled beneath the covers. He thought back on the day: the Threes with the rocks, the lady and the two girls, the sign in the yard. Maybe tomorrow, if he got up the nerve, he would try and get close enough to see what the sign said. But since it was dark and he couldn't do anything until morning anyway, he forced it out of his mind, burrowed deeper under the covers and opened *RATT VOLUME 89: WHAT HAPPENED WHEN THEY GOT CAUGHT.*

CHAPTER 7

LIZZIE WAS SNORING SOFTLY on the couch, exhausted from our strange little trip. I waited until Sophie was engrossed in her pizza and THE HARDEST JIGSAW EVER MADE, then slipped out of the living room and into our bedroom. As I pulled the package from underneath my bed, my hands began to shake. I thought of those divining sticks, the ones that quiver when water is near. What were these shaking hands of mine trying to tell me? What did they already know?

For four years I'd lived in a silent house. Sure there was a chatty Sophie and even Lizzie had the occasional mom thing to say, but we never talked about anything real. Like my dad. Like what happened to him.

I was eight when he died and knew only the bare minimum. That he drowned. That he swam way out and just didn't come back. But I didn't know anything else, like if he'd been alone or with friends; if he'd been in a lake or in the ocean. So I guess with all the silence around it, I'd started to wonder if maybe there was something more. Like maybe he hadn't wanted to come back.

Until that moment my father's death had been the biggest mystery in my life. Now there was another. The house on the island was ours, but why? And who had sent Lizzie the package? And why hadn't she even bothered to open it? *Four years ago.* Maybe it was a coincidence, but I couldn't help but think that these two biggest mysteries in my life were somehow connected.

Something tickled the back of my neck. I reached to brush it off and felt a human finger. I screamed, jumped, and twirled around. "Sophie!" I yelled, relieved it was her. "You scared me!"

Sophie grinned and nodded at the package in my hand. "What's that?" she asked. Her chin was shiny with pizza grease.

"Can't I have some privacy?"

"It's my room, too." Along with "I'll tell Mom," that was Sophie's favorite line. "What is it?" she asked again.

"I don't know what it is, Sophie. It's just a package I found—"

"At the house?"

"Yes."

"Open it up."

"I don't want to right now."

"I'll tell Mom."

"Shut up, Sophie."

Sophie opened her mouth wide and I knew what would follow—a piercing scream that could wake even our sleeping mother. I quickly slapped my hand over her mouth. "Okay," I said, trying to think fast. "But not right now."

"Why not?" she asked. With my hand covering her mouth it sounded like "Bly wot?"

"Because," I said. Sometimes that worked with little sisters.

Sophie thought for a moment. "Blarget?"

"What?"

"Wis ib wubut wur wad?"

"I don't know, Sophie." I took my hand away. Since she was asking about Dad, I knew she wouldn't be calling for Mom.

"Is it about our dad?" she asked again.

"Why would you think that?"

She shrugged. "I don't know," she said. "The house today. Mom not telling us about the sign. You know." I nodded and glanced down at the package. *Four years ago.*

Sophie was getting restless. She tried to snatch it from my hands. "Let's open it and find out," she said. "Maybe it's candy."

"No," I said, clutching it to my chest. "Let's wait." I was dying to open the package, but didn't want Sophie there when I did. It could be anything. It could be something terrible. It could be something she'd tell Lizzie, something that would truly put our mother over the edge. Plus, even though it had my mother's name on it, I felt it was mine. And I wanted to be the first to see what was inside. "We'll do it tomorrow. After school."

"Why not now?"

"Because I don't want to."

Sophie leaned close and stared straight into my eyes. "Promise you won't do it without me?"

I looked away, nodded, and shoved the package underneath my bed. "Let's go finish the pizza, okay? I'll help you with your puzzle."

Sophie has this thing—it's like she's a human alarm clock. I don't know how she discovered she had it, but it is one of her greatest talents. She calls it "setting her head," and this is how it works. Every night, before she falls asleep, my sister will ask, "What time should I set my head for, Margaret?"

"Seven, Sophie," I always say, and she then proceeds to set her head for seven o'clock. According to Sophie, if you want to wake up at seven, picture the number seven on the face of a giant clock in the middle of the desert. ("It has to be a desert, Margaret, or it doesn't work," she once told me.) Watch that clock until the little hand hits seven and the big hand hits twelve, setting off a huge, gonging alarm. Let the alarm gong seven times and the next morning, according to my sister, "Your eyes will just pop open at the right time exactly!" I tried it once, but we just ended up being late for school. Lizzie can't do it either. So, for as long as I can remember, we've both just depended on Sophie to get us up in the morning. And she's never failed. Not once.

That night, like every other, Sophie snuggled

under her covers and asked, "What time should I set my head for, Margaret?" I told her seven, then waited until I heard her slow, steady, sleeping breath. Sophie can slide into sleep as easily as a cat. I waited a few more minutes, just to be sure she was asleep enough, then I reached under my bed and felt around for the package. It wasn't there.

"You'll never find it." I could hear the smug smile in my sister's sleepy little voice.

"I'll kill you," I said.

"Then you'll really never find it. Why'd you lie to me?"

"Because it's my package."

"No it's not. It's Mom's. You want to open it now, Margaret? I'll show you where it is."

"Shut up," I said.

"Okay," she said, "maybe I'll let you tomorrow." Then she rolled over, sighed softly and, quick as that, was in her deep, sweet sleep.

CHAPTER 8

"BOYD, HONEY, HURRY OR you'll miss breakfast again!" his mother shouted from the kitchen. Boyd smelled something cooking and, for one wonderful moment, thought it might be pancakes and bacon. Then he remembered.

He grabbed his backpack and his jacket. If he timed it just right, he'd be able to wait until the school bus pulled in front of his house, then dash through the living room with a quick, "'Bye, Mom, the bus is here," which would save him from another breakfast of bran flakes and tofu sausages.

"Boyd, I mean it," his mom called again. "You need to eat."

"I'll be there in just a minute, Mom!" he shouted back, then stopped in front of the window. "Come on, come on, come on," he whispered, looking down to check his watch. When he looked up again, there it was—the familiar flash of bright yellow. "Bus is coming, gotta go," he shouted gleefully as he ran through the living room, out the front door and across the damp lawn. But that feeling of elation disappeared the moment he stepped onto the bus. Rows of faces stared up at him, and not one of them smiled.

Boyd walked down the aisle and slid into the first empty seat he could find. As the bus lurched forward, he slouched down and turned to the window. As usual, the Threes in the back laughed and directed "rat boy" comments his way. (At twelve, he'd already made the biggest mistake of his life: an impassioned book report on his collection of Ratt books. No one in his class would ever let him forget it.)

"If they only knew," Boyd said to himself, thinking about the Threes and the rocks and the boys from the comic book. Suddenly he remembered something else—the lady and the truck and the two girls—and he turned to look for the sign they'd left in the yard. As the bus rolled past, Boyd pressed his face against the window for a closer look at the mansion, which was just as dark and imposing as ever. In fact, nothing about it had changed in the slightest. The sign was gone.

CHAPTER 9

I DON'T KNOW IF you've heard about it, but there's a pack of wild Chihuahuas traveling up through Mexico. Most people think of Chihuahuas as those miniature yappy dogs that old women dress as babies, but these Chihuahuas—they are wild and they are mean and they travel in a pack, just like wolves. They've already crossed the desert and are now heading north, killing any living thing that gets in their way. Every morning, when I walk Sophie to school and watch her run across the playground to join her squirmy little friends, I think about that dog pack.

"So we'll open the package after school today, right, Margaret?" It was Monday morning and Sophie and I stood next to the chain-link fence that encircled her school.

"Whatever," I said. Earlier, while Sophie was in the kitchen eating her cereal, I had made a quick and desperate search for the package. Nothing.

"It's not a big deal," I added, hoping that by after school that day she might forget.

Sophie smiled knowingly and gave me a quick wave. Then she turned and ran across the playground, her little feet kicking up a cloud of dirt and gravel. I continued down the sidewalk, three blocks to Holy Names Academy.

If watching Sophie's classmates is like watching a pack of miniature dogs, watching my own is like watching one of Lizzie's nature programs—the one where the gorillas or the chimpanzees strut around trying to figure out who is leader. At Holy Names everyone wears a uniform. Three months before, when I first heard I was being transferred to a uniform school, I was secretly pleased—no more trying to fit in by wearing the right jeans, hurrah. But after my first day there, I realized that even though we were all supposed to look the same in our white shirts and navy skirts or slacks, we really didn't look the same at all—just like gorillas don't look the same to other gorillas.

That morning, like every morning, I stood outside the chain-link fence and waited for the third and final bell to ring. And as I watched my classmates chase each other, throw balls back and forth, and talk in little groups, I pictured the pack of wild Chihuahuas that could appear at any moment—all the way from Mexico and not even out of breath. They would run along the chain-link fence, searching for a way to get inside so they could shred us all to meatloaf.

When the third bell rang, I turned and looked down the street. No Chihuahuas. "You're all safe for today," I said out loud to no one. Then I stepped onto the playground and followed the girls with their smooth legs (intact) and boys with their wiry arms (intact) toward the double-door entrance to our school.

My mind had wandered back home, found the package and was just about to open it up when Mr. Homeroom called my name. I jumped, even though I'd known it was coming.

"Margaret," he said again, "enlighten us with your knowledge."

I stood up slowly and walked to the front of the room, dragging my poster-board collage behind me. We'd been working on these reports and posters for two weeks, but until that very moment, I hadn't realized how different mine looked from everyone else's.

I placed my poster on the stand and cleared my throat. The words I'd been rehearsing for days must have come out in the right order, but only when I got to the end did I actually start to hear what I was saying. "And so, in conclusion, no one really knows why animal attacks are on the rise. For wild animals, it makes sense because we're crowding them out of their natural spaces. But for domesticated animals like Chihuahuas, no one really knows for sure."

I looked up to thirty kids, sixty eyes, staring blankly at my poster-board collage of people who, while playing in public parks, had lost eyes, noses, and large chunks of legs to ferrets, raccoons, runaway dogs—even birds. My poster board was so full of teeth marks and gaping wounds that there wasn't even room for my world map locating killer bee swarms. For the first time since starting my project, I was thankful for that.

Mr. Homeroom clapped his hands together as he always did when he didn't know what else to do. "Okay," he said, "questions. Question time. Any, um . . . questions?"

D.J., who sat in the back because he was taller than everyone else, raised his hand. "Go ahead, D.J.," said Mr. Homeroom.

"I thought this was supposed to be about tornadoes and earthquakes. Or like asteroids and tectonic plates."

"It's supposed to be on a topic in nature that interests you," answered Mr. Homeroom. I could tell he was choosing his words carefully.

"But I thought you said scientific things. Like, that are real." A few kids laughed. And they weren't laughing at D.J. No one ever laughed at D.J., king of the right sneakers.

"Margaret," prompted Mr. Homeroom, "would you like to defend your report as scientific?"

I could feel my face getting hot. If I pretended to faint, would they wheel me out on a gurney? "Not really," I said.

"Why not?" asked Mr. Homeroom.

"Because—" I looked out the window. Was that them in the distance—a line of tiny beige dogs waiting patiently for recess? "Because," I said finally, "people believe what they want to believe." I forced my eyes away from the window and turned back to see D.J. staring at me. I willed myself not to blink. Or look away. Or throw up. Suddenly D.J. looked down at his hands. I'd won.

Mr. Homeroom cleared his throat. "Okay," he said. "Well, thank you, Margaret. Very provocative photographs."

I picked up the poster and walked back to my desk, my face still burning hot. I glanced out the window again, looking for the Chihuahua pack, but there was nothing. Nothing was there.

CHAPTER 10

P.E. PHYSICAL EDUCATION. Whoever came up with the idea must have hated kids. The week's sport was baseball, and as I suited up, I took long, deep breaths to calm myself. Once, during soccer week, I got so nervous I hyperventilated and had to go to the nurse. The rest of that week, whenever I stepped out onto the playing field, my classmates grabbed their throats and gasped for air. Ha, ha.

Mrs. P.E. had her clipboard tucked underneath her arm—a sign that, once again, I had missed the team assignments and batting orders. "What team am I on?" I asked, shuffling up to her and hoping she'd say, "Too late. Sorry. Sit this one out."

Instead she pointed to the team at bat. "You need to start being on time, Margaret. You're fifth up."

Slowly I made my way to the dugout.

D.J. stood on the pitcher's mound, tossing the ball around to the other infielders, who were all expert in that certain kind of baseball chatter that seems as much a part of spring as chirping birds and wind chimes. (Around the horn, D.J., attaboy! Pitch it here, buddy, nice toss.)

"Let's go," shouted Mrs. P.E., clapping her hands loudly. "Play ball!"

D.J. stomped on the pitcher's mound and cupped

his hand around the ball. The first batter was tall and muscular and, like D.J., looked like he was born with a gym bag slung over his shoulder.

D.J. did his famous high-leg windup, then twisted his body, swung his arm, and sent the ball flying. The batter swayed his hips, adjusted his arms, and waited, waited, waited. He continued to hold the bat, poised and ready, even as the ball reached the plate. Then, just when I thought it was too late, he tightened his grip and swung the bat in a smooth, powerful stroke.

The bat connected with the ball, making a beautiful, loud crack. The batter sprang forward and ran down the first-base line, his arms and legs pumping like a powerful new machine.

"Get him out," I whispered. The ball landed a few yards over third base, but by the time the shortstop scooped it up and threw it to the girl on first, it was too late—he was already there, breathing easily and clapping for the next batter to bring him on home. Unless the next three batters went out one, two, three, I would have to bat that inning.

The next two batters hit pop flies, but then a girl hit the ball so far she made it to second base, putting a runner on third. So with two outs and runners on second and third, I picked up the bat and made that long, painful walk to home plate.

"Bat off your shoulder," Mrs. P.E. yelled as I positioned myself in the batter's box.

I lifted the bat slightly and squinted across to the

pitcher's mound. From the dugout I heard one of my teammates say, "I bet she's going for the walk again."

"Ball one!" shouted Mrs. P.E. as the first pitch flew across the plate.

"You're right," said another. "She is."

"Ball two!"

My teammates were right—I *was* going for the walk. It was easier than swinging, missing, and having to walk back to the bench with everyone watching.

D.J. rubbed the ball into his mitt, then looked up. Even with the sun shining in his face, he managed to look me straight in the eye. The stare-down that had started earlier in Mr. Homeroom's class was on again. I hadn't won the war, after all.

D.J. raised his arm and tossed the ball—no spin, no speed, just a nice, easy lob. *How can you not swing at me?* this pitch seemed to say. The ball floated over the plate, then at the very last moment, veered slightly to the left. The bat never moved from my shoulder.

"Ball three!" shouted Mrs. P.E. "Bat off your shoulder, Margaret."

"How does she want it? Dipped in chocolate?" someone asked from the dugout and everyone laughed.

I shifted my stance ever so slightly and tried to ignore them. Just one more, I said to myself. Just one more ball and I'd be able to walk to first.

"That's a strike!" shouted Mrs. P.E. as the next ball

flew across the plate. Then, "Strike two!"

"Come on, D.J. You can do it." My own team was actually cheering for him—could anything be worse? I glanced around the field, praying for a rainstorm, an earthquake, my Chihuahua pack. Anything.

D.J.'s neck was bright red and his lips were pressed together so tightly they were almost white—a sign that maybe he was more nervous than I'd realized. That gave me an idea.

As D.J. wound up and was about to release the ball, I raised my head and grinned at him. It was the biggest smile my mouth could manage. And you know what? It worked. D.J. was so startled that the ball slipped from his fingers and practically rolled across home plate. Before Mrs. P.E. had a chance to yell "Ball four!" I'd already dropped my bat and was on my way to first.

I won't bore you with many more baseball details, except that the next batter "went out swinging," as they say. Of course, everyone shouted things like, "At least you tried," and "Better to swing and miss than not swing at all." I jogged back to the bench and grabbed my mitt, pretending not to hear the words that were really meant for me.

The outfield. The outfield wasn't as bad as being up to bat, but it had the potential to be. I always played way out, as far out as the teacher allowed. This meant I rarely saw any action, but when I did, it was usually big action. That's why every pitch, every swing, every *thwack* of the bat made my heart leap like a wild animal trapped in a cramped cage.

I crouched over my knees like I'd seen professional baseball players do. The key to the outfield was to look like you were ready—then you weren't such an obvious target. Just a few feet away from me, a girl was doing handstands. That was dangerous. A really good hitter could see that as a hole in the defense and send a ball flying our way.

"You'd better at least look like you're playing," I said to her. I'd never spoken to her before, but I knew her name was Tina Louise.

"Why?" she asked, her voice muffled from being upside down.

I didn't have time to explain. "You just should."

At that moment I heard a loud crack. A girl in the infield ran, dove, and caught the ball just inches from the ground.

"Some people are born with absolutely everything they will ever need," I heard Tina Louise say. I glanced over at her. She was on two feet now, watching the girl throw the ball back to the pitcher.

"Oh well," she added after a moment. Her wild, frizzy hair had slipped out of its clasp, and she tied it back before kicking into another perfect handstand. "Can you do this?" she upside-down asked.

I shook my head, then realized she couldn't see me. "No," I said.

"Have you ever tried?"

"No," I said.

"Then how do you know you can't do it?"

I wanted to say, "Because it's not a natural human thing to do," but stopped myself. Instead I looked at home plate. Now D.J. was up, shuffling his feet and squeezing his hands around the base of the bat. He straightened slightly, looked to the outfield and pointed his bat directly at me. *Now it's your turn*, he seemed to be saying.

"You'd better get ready," I said to Tina Louise. "Really, I mean it."

She shifted her weight slightly to the right and lifted her left arm, more steady on one hand than most people are on two feet. "No one ever hits it out here," she said.

"He might this time," I whispered, mostly to myself.

Just then the loudest baseball crack I'd ever heard echoed across the field. I don't know much about baseball, but I do know that this ball and this bat connected in a perfect way. I could tell by the sound.

I shaded my eyes from the sun and looked for the ball. I spotted it finally, flying like some living thing— a wonderful living thing that had been held against its will inside a white leather shell, then set free by one perfect kiss of the bat.

For a moment I believed it would fly off to a secret place in the sky—a secret place where the few, lucky, set-free balls go. But then it seemed to change its mind. Maybe freedom wasn't what it was after—

maybe it really liked to play baseball—because what happened was, it started to turn and swoop. It started to fly in my direction.

Move, my brain said, *get ready and move*. But I was frozen watching it. The birds and the grass and the trees were frozen watching it. Everyone was frozen watching it—everyone except Tina Louise, who was just coming out of her one-handed handstand. And as her feet touched the grass and her arms shot up in an *I'm on TV* pose, *SMACK*—the ball hit her forehead and Tina Louise dropped. Straight as a plank, without a sound, flat on her back, out cold.

The entire field remained frozen for a moment, then erupted into shouts of fear and joy and confusion. Like ants to their first sticky piece of candy, my classmates swarmed in, riled and excited, but not quite sure what to do with this new thing.

Since I was already right there, I had a moment alone to study her face. It was a face with nothing on it—no fear or laughter or question or dream or anything. Just pure face. Tina Louise seemed to have disappeared into her own world, but where was that world? Where did she go?

As the other kids crowded around, their running shouts trickled to complete silence. Together we stood in a tight circle, staring down at the peaceful face of our fallen classmate, who looked as close to dead as any of us had ever seen. The world stopped moving and was so quiet that I actually heard a leaf scoot across the playfield. And then, far away, the tinkle of chimes. Wind chimes meant a neighborhood somewhere, with a house and a back porch and a retired couple out watering their begonias—two people who didn't know that Tina Louise had been knocked unconscious by a baseball. How funny that the entire world didn't know this was happening.

We stood there, waiting for what would come next. And what came next was this: A small wet spot appeared on Tina Louise's shorts. The spot grew and spread until it was a large wet stain.

It couldn't be happening, but it was.

Tina Louise was peeing her pants.

And then suddenly, with no flicker or flutter or warning at all, her eyes opened wide—blank and staring—and a flood of tears poured down her cheeks. It was as if the tears had been there all along, building up behind closed eyelids, having nothing to do with emotion at all. Like her body knew it should cry but her mind hadn't caught up with it yet.

Our circle was suddenly broken by Mrs. P.E., who knelt down beside Tina Louise and touched her head. And that's when Tina Louise's mind caught up with the tears. Her eyes tried to focus. Her face turned red. She choked out a scared sob, then another.

"Okay, you kids," Mrs. P.E. said sternly, "clear out. And somebody run and get Mary Jane."

Nobody moved.

"Now!" she said. "Someone get Mary Jane!"

We all stood fixed to the ground, watching Tina Louise's face grow more splotchy and red with each new and wrenching sob. Mrs. P.E. pulled off her sweatshirt and draped it over Tina Louise's wet shorts. "Get Mary Jane Johnson!" she repeated. "Get her now."

Again, nobody moved. We didn't know what to do. Finally one brave voice asked the question for all of us. "Um, who is Mary Jane Johnson?"

Mrs. P.E. squinted up at us, just as confused. "What?"

"We don't know who Mary Jane Johnson is."

Her face got ready to pop. "Nurse!" she shouted at us. "Nurse Johnson!"

Of course, we all seemed to be nodding in relief, *Nurse Johnson*. With one last look at Tina Louise, still groggy-eyed and wet all over, my classmates scattered across the playground, running, leaping, shouting. We'd just seen something we had no words for, and the image of Tina Louise—flat on her back and peeing her pants—would be forever branded in our minds.

CHAPTER 11

SOMETIMES I THINK ABOUT how things might have been different. What if Tina Louise hadn't been knocked out by that baseball? Or what if she hadn't been standing next to me? What if she'd been standing next to someone who would have reached out and caught it? I get scared when I think about it, because you know what? The way it all happened meant that for the first time since transferring to Holy Names Academy, I actually spoke to another human being—someone besides my mother, my sister, and the man who gives us change at the Laundromat.

Here's how it happened. After school that day, I stood behind a big fir tree, waiting for the buses to pull out. I wasn't hiding, exactly, I just didn't want anyone to see me. A tap on my shoulder made me jump. "Don't you ride the bus?" It was Tina Louise, standing there with a white bandage strapped around her head.

"No," I said, catching my breath. I glanced down at my shoes, then at my hands holding the animal-attack poster. I didn't know what to say.

"Well, then, are you waiting for the buses to leave?" she asked.

I nodded.

"Me, too," she said.

I looked up at her, wanting to ask things like, "Do you hide from the buses every day or just today?" and "Where did you go when you were knocked out like that?" Instead I said, "Are you okay?"

Tina Louise rocked back and forth on her heels as the buses began pulling out of the lot. She was watching them, but she was also somewhere else, and I was pretty sure she hadn't heard me.

"I should have tried to catch it," I said when the silence started making me nervous.

"No," she said slowly, dreamily, coming back to her rocking feet. "It was meant for me. It was Fate. For whatever reason, I was marked." She didn't look at me when she said it, but kept her eyes on the line of buses. When the last one pulled away, she started to walk. "Okay," she said, "let's go."

I followed her across the empty lot. "Why didn't you go home afterward?" My voice sounded funny— high pitched and slow like I was talking to an ancient aunt or a wobbly toddler.

"No one was home. The nurse watched me for an hour to make sure I wouldn't go into a coma."

I thought about Tina Louise in a coma, asleep for the rest of her life, not hearing, not seeing, and being fed from a tube. Dead and alive at the same time. "Hmmm," I said nervously. "So now you won't go into a coma?"

Tina Louise shrugged. "The nurse said I seemed fine. She called my mom."

We walked along the sidewalk like we knew exactly where the other was going, like we did this every day. All afternoon I'd been thinking of this question, wanting to ask her this question. Now was my chance. I cleared my throat several times and finally it came out. "Tina Louise," I said. "What was it like? Being knocked out like that?"

She thought for a moment. "Like nothing," she said slowly. "I didn't even know I was hit."

We were both silent then, but for some reason it didn't seem awkward or embarrassing. As we turned the corner, Sophie's school came into view. I slowed my pace.

"I'm different now," Tina Louise said suddenly.

"What do you mean?"

"Now, whenever anyone looks at me, they'll see me like that. You know. Peeing my pants."

I wanted to laugh and cry. I wanted to bark. "That's not true," I said, even though I knew it was.

"It's not like I was extremely popular or anything before," she continued. "But now, well. At least I'll know what to expect."

Tina Louise was right—she wasn't popular or unpopular. More like a quirky piece of furniture you get so used to having around, you forget about seeing.

But I wasn't thinking about that. Something she said had stuck in my mind. "What you said about Fate—"

"Yes," she said. "You saw the ball. It came straight at me."

I remembered D.J. pointing the bat directly at my head. "But what if it was really meant for someone else?" I asked. Doesn't that mean something? Doesn't that mean something about *their* Fate? That ball was meant for me and I knew it.

Tina Louise stopped and turned to me. "You don't know anything about Fate, do you? When I'm thirty years old I'll look back on this day as a turning point. This day changed my life. Everyone has a day like that."

I thought back to the day before—the trip to the island and the package waiting for me at home. "How will this day have changed your life?" We were face-to-face on the sidewalk and the world was holding its breath, waiting for her to answer.

"I don't know just yet. But it will. Like maybe someone who used to want to be my friend won't want to be my friend anymore. And maybe that person is someone who I would have gone driving around with when we turned sixteen. But because we're not friends, I won't be in the car. And maybe they crash and die. And I'm still alive. That's just an example."

"All because of one little thing?"

"My mother says for every action, there's a reaction. You didn't even know my name until today, did you?"

I hesitated. "Well, I knew your name. I knew who you were."

She smiled knowingly. "But we'd never talked before, had we?" She turned and started walking again.

"Honestly," I said, running to catch up, "I've never talked to anyone at this school."

"But now you are."

"Yes."

Tina Louise raised her hands, like she was holding something important for me to see. "That's Fate, right? You and me, standing in the outfield. Neither one of us could catch a ball to save our lives. You see?"

We were in front of Sophie's school. I stopped walking and scanned the playground. There was Sophie, playing by herself. All the other kids had already gone home. "My sister," I said apologetically as she dropped from the monkey bars and came running.

"Oh, well," said Tina Louise. "I actually live the other way. See you tomorrow."

"Okay," I said. I watched her turn and walk back in the direction of the school. "Tina Louise," I called out—and I heard things in my voice. Gratitude, fear, hope.

"Yes?" She spun around and waited.

"See you tomorrow."

Tina Louise raised her arm in a farewell salute. "By the way," she called, "I liked your report."

"What?"

"The Chihuahuas. I thought it was very relevant."

I grinned as she lowered her arm, spun back around and continued on her way.

"Who was that?" Sophie asked, bouncing up next to me with her tongue hanging out of her mouth.

"Tina Louise," I said. "Put your tongue back in your mouth."

"I thought you didn't have any friends." She tugged on my arm.

I ignored Sophie and watched Tina Louise slowly make her way down the sidewalk. Occasionally she would reach up and gently pat her bandaged head. When she came to the corner, she stopped, turned to me and raised her arm once again. It was something I'd been waiting for and hadn't even known it. I felt like laughing. I felt like jumping. I raised my arm high above my head and waved back.

"She's not looking anymore—you can put your arm down," said Sophie after Tina Louise had turned and disappeared around the corner.

"Here, let's take the elevator," I said. We were standing in front of our apartment building. The excitement of Tina Louise had pushed the package out of my mind for most of the afternoon, but now it was back. And my heart was racing at the thought of it.

Sophie glanced at me sideways. "Mom said we should always take the stairs. The elevator is for old people who can't walk."

"There aren't any old people waiting, are there?

You can push the buttons."

"Okay," she said.

I knew I had to keep Sophie distracted long enough to find the package and open it on my own. So far, the story about Tina Louise had put everything else out of her mind. ("So she really peed her pants in front of everyone?" "Yes, Sophie." "Real pee? Actual pee?" "Real pee, Sophie.") Pushing the buttons on the elevator was another good diversion.

"Do you want to unlock the door?" I asked, handing her my key.

Sophie grinned. "Okay," she said, unlocking the door and stepping inside. Then she looked around quizzically, like she knew there was something important to do but couldn't remember what it was.

"Hey," I said quickly, before she could remember, "how far are you on your puzzle? Can you tell what the picture is yet?"

Sophie, completely taken by surprise at my first ever interest in her jigsaw, ran to the corner of the living room. "Look," she said. "I thought I saw the tip of a finger this morning."

I joined her in the corner. "Oh, yeah, that does look like a finger," I said. I picked up a tiny piece from the floor and pretended to search for a fit. Sophie snatched it from my hand and, a moment later, was deep in her jigsaw trance. "I'll go get us a snack," I said, but she didn't seem to hear me.

I tiptoed out of the living room and down the hall

to our bedroom. I shut and locked the door, hung my backpack on the arm of my chair and tossed my poster board in the corner. I knew I had to be quick.

I stood in the middle of the room and tried to do the impossible: think like Sophie. First I checked underneath her bed. Nothing. I looked in her drawers, then gave her more credit than she deserved and looked in mine. Nothing.

I sat down on the edge of the bed and glanced around the room. The closet. I pulled open the closet door and kicked through the piles of clothes that never managed to make it to the Laundromat. Nothing. What if it wasn't even in the bedroom? Would Sophie have tried to outsmart me by hiding it in the kitchen? The living room? Our mother's room?

I knew the answer the minute I heard Sophie's frantic voice at the door. "Margaret!" she called. "You can't open it without me." Okay, so the package *was* in the bedroom. I took another look around. "Margaret!" she called again, her voice on the verge of a scream. "You have to let me in. No locked doors, Mom said. And it's my room, too."

"Just a minute, Sophie," I said. "I just want a few minutes of privacy." To the rhythmic beat of Sophie's fist I went into fast-motion search. "Think like Sophie, think like Sophie," I muttered to myself as I tore the room apart. Nothing—and I'd looked everywhere.

As I made my way to the door, ready to admit

defeat, I brushed against my backpack hanging from the arm of the chair. Could Sophie be that smart? I grabbed it and unzipped the top to the main compartment. There was my notebook and math book and crumpled-up sack from my lunch—but something felt different. I opened the zipper to an inside compartment, one that I never use, and there it was. I must have carried it with me the whole day and hadn't even known!

My genius sister was suddenly quiet on the other side of the door. "Sophie?" I said. Was she in telling Mom? "Sophie?" I said again and waited. Waited, waited.

"What?" she said finally.

"I'll be out in a second, okay?"

"Did you find it?"

"No, Sophie. I looked everywhere. I know it must be in another room."

Even though there was a locked door between us, I could tell she was grinning. "Then what are you *doing* in there, Margaret?"

"Just stuff. Stuff you do when you're twelve," I answered.

"Like bras and stuff?"

I glanced down at my flat chest. "Maybe."

"Can I see?"

"Just give me five minutes of privacy, okay?"

And even though there was a locked door between us, I could tell she was nodding.

Five minutes in Sophie time is about forty-three seconds in the real world. I could hear her on the other side of the door, fiddling with the carpet and humming a Sophie song. Quietly, I lifted the package from my backpack. I turned it over in my hands, even though I knew I didn't have any time to waste. *Why couldn't I open it? What was I afraid of?*

At any moment I expected to hear Sophie shout, "Margaret, it's been five minutes!" or even, "Margaret! Why is your heart beating so *loud*?" I took a deep breath and tore the package open. Then, without looking, I reached inside and let my fingers pull out the first thing they touched. I stared at it for several moments, not quite believing but not completely surprised, either.

In my hand was a book, a comic-type book with a hand-drawn cover. The title was the longest I'd ever seen: *RATT VOLUME 1: HOW TO DISAPPEAR COMPLETELY AND NEVER BE FOUND*. But it wasn't the words that made my stomach flutter—it was the drawing. On the cover was a picture of the house. The island house. The For Sale by Owner house.

"Margaret?" Sophie started to scratch on the other side of the door. "Margaret, Margaret, Margaret?"

I reached into the package again and felt my fingers close around something small and hard. I pulled it out. It was a key. An old, rusted key.

"Margaret! It's been a long time. A very long time."

"Okay, Sophie." Hands shaking, I held the package upside down and dumped out the final item—a first-place medal tied to a faded blue silk ribbon. On the front of the medal was the raised figure of a swimmer, caught in mid-dive. I turned it over and read the name engraved on the back. Jack Clairmont. My father's name.

"Margaret, this is your last chance!" Sophie called. Quickly I replaced the medal, the key and the comic, then shoved the package into the secret compartment of my backpack.

"Right there, Sophie," I said, hanging the pack on the back of the chair. I unlocked the door and Sophie pushed inside, her nose in the air like a suspicious poodle.

"You shouldn't lock the door," was all she said, but I watched her eyes study the backpack. Finally, she let out a relieved sigh and turned back to me. "You want me to show you where the package is?"

"No," I said. "I'm going to do my homework."

"Then I'm opening it myself."

"Then I'll tell Mom," I said, stealing her line. It was perfect and she knew it. There was nothing she could say back.

Sophie spent the rest of the evening watching me out of the corner of her eye. Every time I reached into my backpack, she held her breath. I sat on the living room floor and pretended to do my math homework, but really all I was doing was scribbling down, over and over, the three things I'd found. A comic book, a key, and a swimming medal. Every time I thought of the swimming medal I got the same funny feeling on the back of my neck, like someone was tickling it with a feather.

My drowned father, the swim champ.

CHAPTER 12

BOYD CLOSED THE BOOK and shivered. He'd already read the story three times straight through and was now revisiting his favorite parts. This was the latest Ratt adventure, and in it the Drowning Ghost was more menacing than ever. In just a few nights the full moon would bring the ghost out once again, and he would roam the waters searching for a new pair of eyes.

Snuggling deeper into the covers, Boyd closed his eyes. "Something was rocking the boat," he whispered, pretending to be one of the fishermen. Soon he would feel the icy finger of the Drowning Ghost on the back of his neck; a moment later he'd be pulled over the side of the boat and dragged down, down, down. Down to the bottom of the sea.

CHAPTER 13

ONCE YOU KNOW HOW to spot a pack, you start to see them everywhere, especially in the school lunchroom. That's why the safest place to eat lunch is in a bathroom stall. It might not sound very appetizing, but it is the safest.

The day after I opened the package, the day after Tina Louise had been knocked unconscious by the baseball, I was in my favorite stall (second from the left), sitting on the toilet seat eating a slice of leftover pepperoni pizza and examining the first-place swimming medal hanging around my neck. *A swimming medal, a key, a comic with the house on the cover.* I was so lost in trying to make sense of the three things I'd found that I jumped when I heard the main door to the rest room slam open and shut. I stopped chewing and peeked through the crack of my stall.

There she was, Tina Louise, bent over the sink and doing something as ordinary as washing her hands. I watched her straighten up and tear off a piece of paper towel, all the while examining her face and the white bandage still strapped to her head.

Tucking the medal back inside my shirt, I did something I didn't know I was going to. "Hey," I said. I unlocked the bolt and opened the stall door about an inch. "Hey, Tina Louise."

Tina Louise twirled around and then froze. She looked from me to the pizza in my hand to the toilet seat behind me. Now I was stuck. What had I been thinking? Since there was no going back, I did the only thing I could: I opened the door a little wider. The gracious hostess inviting a guest into her newly redecorated home.

Tina Louise took a step forward, still eyeing the pizza suspiciously. When she reached the door she hesitated before slipping inside. I shut the door behind her and locked us in. Then we stood face-to-face and inches apart, trapped. Tina Louise cleared her throat. "Well, hmmm," she said finally, "do you always eat your lunch in here?"

"Not always," I said. Then, "Well, yeah."

Tina Louise looked at the brown-paper bag perched on the back of the toilet seat. She glanced around the pink stall with its scratched-in names and dates. Someone had written a little poem that said, "If you tinkle and you sprinkle, be a sweetie and wipe the seatie." And underneath it, someone else had scrawled, "Make me, you ass wipe."

I was waiting to see what Tina Louise would do. Would she turn against me? Would she call me ass wipe and run out into the hall shouting, "Margaret's eating pizza—*on the toilet!*"

Tina Louise opened her mouth to say something, but at first nothing came out. Then it happened. She started to giggle. It wasn't a laugh like she was laughing at me—it was just a giggle. A nice, friendly giggle.

But what does a person say back to a giggle? Just as I was about to explain my lunchtime routine, the rest room door swung open again.

"Shhh." I put my finger to my lips and motioned to the footsteps on the tile, but the giggles had already taken hold and Tina Louise couldn't stop. I quickly flushed the toilet to cover the sound and peered through the crack in the stall. Two girls in front of the mirror, side by side, with combs and lip gloss. Trouble.

"It smells like meat in here," said one of the girls.

"Disgusting," said the other. I saw their eyes meet in the mirror and a subtle nod of their heads.

I glanced over at Tina Louise. Her face was flushed, her cheeks were bulging and, as I watched her stuff her hand into her mouth to keep from making a sound, my fear suddenly turned into something else— something I hadn't felt in a long time. Biting the back of my hand, I tried to think of sad things, scary things, ugly things, but it was no use. I, too, had the giggles.

I flushed the toilet once again, but already it was too late. I looked up as a shadow fell over me. The two girls had climbed onto the toilet seat in the next stall and were staring down at us. Us in a bathroom stall with pepperoni pizza.

For what felt like a really long time, no one said a word. Then it came. "Gross," said one of the girls. She said it calmly, matter-of-factly, like she was looking down on two disgusting bugs doing some disgusting bug thing.

"Gross," confirmed the other.

I grabbed my lunch sack from the back of the toilet seat and unbolted the stall door. "Come on," I said to Tina Louise. Her face was still flushed, but I don't think it was from the giggles anymore. Heads high, we marched to the door of the rest room. I tossed my lunch in the garbage on the way out.

Tina Louise followed me through the crowded hallway to the main doors of the school. I walked like I knew where I was going, even though I had no idea. I wondered what people thought when they saw us together. *There goes the Chihuahua girl. There goes Pee-Pee Pants.*

When I found myself out on the playfield, I stopped and turned to face her. I wanted to say something, but what could I say? All I could think about was the look on the girls' faces as they caught us huddled together in the stall. "Gross," I said.

Tina Louise looked at me a moment, then started to laugh. At first it was just a nervous little ha-ha, but then something caught hold of her. Whatever it was, it caught hold of me, too, and all at once we were laughing for real. We laughed and laughed until we were both doubled over so far our faces almost touched the ground.

"Oh, no," she choked out between gasps for air. "This might be the second day I pee my pants at school."

And that made us laugh even harder.

I thought about the two girls again. If I'd been alone it wouldn't have been funny at all. I thought about the day before, what had brought us together, and our talk on the way home from school. The swimming medal was suddenly burning a hole in my chest.

"Hey, Tina Louise," I said, "remember what you said yesterday? About Fate?" She nodded, still trying to catch her breath. Just then the bell rang and we both glanced up at the school. As quick as they'd come over us, the giggles were suddenly gone.

"That's just the first bell," Tina Louise said. She looked at me, waiting.

I tried to think of where to start. *See, my mom . . . see, there's this house . . . see, my dad died when I was eight.* Instead I reached into my shirt and pulled out the faded blue ribbon. "I found this," I said. "In a package for my mom."

Tina Louise reached out and took the medal in her hand.

I felt my throat tighten. The second bell was about to ring. "See," I squeaked, "my dad was a champion swimmer. I never knew that." I stopped. I cleared my throat and looked at the ground.

Tina Louise let go of the medal and it thumped

against my chest. "Oh," she said, waiting for something more.

"My dad died four years ago. My mom won't talk about it." Kids were rushing past us, trying to get to class before the tardy bell rang. How could I explain it when I didn't even understand it? "See, what happened was, my dad drowned." I heard the words before I knew I was going to say them, and once they were out, I couldn't get them back.

Tina Louise reached over and touched the medal again, this time looking closely at the raised figure of the swimmer. "So," she said finally, and I could hear all the other words behind it.

"Yes," I said.

"You want me to come over after school today?"

I smiled, nodded, and tucked the medal back inside my shirt. "We can still beat the bell," I said. Together we turned and raced to class.

CHAPTER 14

FOR BOYD THE BEST part of the school day was lunchtime. While the other kids gathered around long tables, sniffed sandwiches and traded desserts, Boyd made himself invisible just long enough to sneak past the chain-link fence that encircled the school grounds. Only when he was out of sight of the brick building did he feel free to take his first real breath of the day.

Boyd usually managed to choke down a few bites of his spinach and tofu roll-up during the ten-minute walk into town. Then, if he had enough change, he would stop in at the drugstore for a candy bar or a cherry-filled donut. But lunch for Boyd wasn't really about food. It was about the library.

The island had two libraries. One was called the Bookbus—a library on wheels that came over on the ferry twice a month and parked on Main Street. The Bookbus was crammed with all types of books and even took special orders. The drivers were always nice and liked to talk about authors and illustrators, and some were even known to stop along the side of the road for a waving pedestrian, just like a taxi.

The second library was a bright yellow building in the middle of town, conceived and run by a small man with an enormous mustache who would only answer to the name Mr. Librarian.

Editor's Note:

I think it would be useful to insert a brief history of the library here. When Mr. Librarian first moved to the island to open the library, the islanders were thrilled. People lined the street, eager to get a glimpse of the island's first library without wheels. Once the doors opened, however, and they began pulling books from the shelves, their excitement turned to confusion. Under D was not one novel by Dickens. H had no Hawthorne and F had no Frost. There was no Hemingway or Fitzgerald, no Eliot or Kuo. Instead they found stack after stack of handmade books. Some were typed, some were scribbled, some were printed out on cheap computer paper, some were stapled, some had brads, some were held together with twine.

"The unpublished works of Everyman," exclaimed Mr. Librarian proudly. "Everywoman and Everykid, too."

"But what if I want to research what kinds of roses to plant in my yard?" asked one of the confused islanders.

"Look under F for flowers," said Mr. Librarian, pulling out a 365-page notebook and waving it over his head. "This was written by a local green-thumb who took a photograph of her garden every single day of an entire year. You won't find prettier roses than these."

"Poetry?" asked a big man in a PROPERTY OF ALCATRAZ sweatshirt.

"Most of the best poets have never been published," answered Mr. Librarian pointing to P for poetry. "This is their chance to be heard."

"But who writes all this?" asked Mr. Alcatraz and Mr. Roses and all the other confused people crammed into the small, musty space.

"You do," answered Mr. Librarian. "All of you. I got this batch from leaving announcements on barely one-third of your doorsteps. So all of you— just bring in your unpublished manuscripts and I guarantee they'll find a place in this library." And with that, Mr. Librarian launched into his Opening Ceremony Speech. The bright yellow library was officially open.

It was during Mr. Librarian's Opening Ceremony Speech that Boyd discovered the book that would change his life. Turning the corner on Q, he found himself in the middle of the Rs where his hand found and pulled out a beautifully bound comic book. On the cover was a perfectly detailed drawing of the empty mansion next door. "Who wrote this?" Boyd burst out, catching Mr. Librarian in midsentence.

Mr. Librarian glanced over at Boyd and pursed his lips tightly. His eyes flickered to the comic that Boyd held in trembling hands. "I can't say," he said finally.

Boyd glanced around the room and felt his face

get hot—every single eye was focused on him. Mr. Librarian softened just a bit. "I can't say because I don't know," he said. "That particular book was left on my doorstep, very late at night or very early in the morning. I only know the author by his character's name. Ratt."

Boyd looked down at the book. *Ratt Volume 2*. If there was a two, didn't there have to be a one? "Where's volume 1?"

By this time, almost everyone had used Boyd's diversion to make a quick getaway. Now Mr. Librarian glanced around the nearly empty room and sighed. To the few stragglers who were trying to be polite about sneaking out the door, he said with as much dignity as he could muster, "Excuse me for just one moment, folks. I'll be right back." Then he motioned to Boyd with his long, thin index finger and said, "Come here."

Boyd followed the librarian to his desk at the front of the library. Mr. Librarian opened the top drawer, removed two books and placed them in Boyd's hands. Both were made of the same creamy-white paper with edges that were feather soft to the touch. The ink, too, was the same: vibrant reds, deep blues, glimmering yellows, and bottomless blacks.

"*Ratt Volume 3* and *Ratt Volume 4*. They just arrived early this morning. I left here at midnight and returned at 6 A.M., so sometime between those hours the author dropped them off. Marvelous, aren't they?

I think the paper may be handmade."

Boyd took the book and nodded. "But volume 1—"

The librarian shook his head slowly. "No," he said. "I don't have it. I don't know why."

Boyd fingered the three books in his hand. Maybe the first volume would show up someday. "Can I check them out?"

"One at a time."

"The Bookbus lets us take three."

"Okay, two. But only because it's opening-day special."

Boyd nodded happily, filled out his library card application and spent the rest of the weekend on his bed, wandering through the wonderful, terrible, and truly amazing world of the Ratt.

From that day forward, Boyd visited the library almost every day. Sneaking off the school grounds at lunchtime, he'd make the ten-minute walk into town to return the old volume and check out the new one that would have mysteriously appeared in the night. He'd also stop in after school to reread old volumes, telling his parents he was in a special, extracurricular reading program and catching the sports bus home.

After several months of this, Boyd had come up with a plan. Mr. Librarian had been complaining of an overcrowded R section. ("They just keep coming, at least one new volume every night. I have no more space. No more space.")

"So I was thinking," Boyd said, trying to keep his

voice steady and calm. "I could keep the old ones for you. You know, so you have more room in R. I would keep them safe—I already know exactly where I'd put them."

Mr. Librarian looked at him suspiciously. "I don't know," he said. "What about my other patrons?"

In all the time he'd spent in the library, Boyd had never seen another patron since that awkward opening day. Yes, people did bring in things they'd written, but as far as he could tell, no one ever came in to actually check anything out. "It would be like a second branch," Boyd explained. "An expansion because you're doing so well. And if anyone ever wants to read them, I'll bring them in."

"Hmmm. Like a second branch? Hmmm. I like that. The library is expanding. I need a second branch. Yes, I like that."

And so, bit by bit, whenever the R section became B for bursting, Boyd filled his backpack with old Ratt volumes (careful not to bend any corners) and took them home where he lovingly arranged them in neat stacks in his bedroom closet.

He also started wondering about the abandoned house next door. "Who used to live there, Dad?" he asked his father one day.

His father shrugged. "They were long gone before we moved here."

"But why is it still empty?"

"I don't know, Boyd. It just is."

Boyd asked the librarian. "This house," he said pointing to the cover of the latest Ratt book, "this house where Ratt lives. It's the house next to mine. That old house on Waterfront Road."

Mr. Librarian turned away quickly. "Maybe it just looks like the same house," he said.

"No, it's the same," said Boyd. "I know it's the same. Who used to live there?"

"I don't know."

"You must know. You're the librarian. You have all those old newspapers and official records and things."

"So?"

"So—the person who writes these books. Did he used to live there? Is he really a rat?"

"Too many questions. This is a library, remember? You're disturbing my other patrons."

Boyd looked around. As usual, he was the only one in the place. "Just tell me—"

"Listen!" The librarian's voice was stern and hushed. "Do you like the stories?"

Boyd nodded. How could he describe how much he liked the stories? Loved the stories. Lived for the stories.

Mr. Librarian narrowed his eyes and perched on the edge of the desk. "Why?" he asked. He examined Boyd from head to toe, as if truly seeing him for the first time.

Boyd shrugged. How could he explain that the Ratt had changed his life? "I don't know," he said finally, slowly. He took a deep breath. He'd never talked to anyone about Ratt before, and something about it felt new and exciting. "I guess it's because he started out like an ordinary kid. He didn't have many friends, you know, because he looked a little different. Then, when it started to happen—you know, the hair and stuff—he was even more of an outcast. But, see, it wasn't really a terrible thing after all, what he turned into. Because he made it into a good thing." Boyd looked down at his hands and shrugged.

The librarian cleared his throat. "Interesting interpretation," he said. "But how is becoming one of the most disgusting creatures on the planet a good thing? In your opinion, I mean."

"Well," Boyd answered thoughtfully, "he's brave now. He's not afraid of anyone. He turns garbage into treasure. I don't know. I can't explain it any better. People would die for that treasure, like in volume 27, but it's just the stuff they threw out a month before. People don't see the good in something if it's not perfect. But he does." Boyd stopped. He wasn't even quite sure what he'd just said. How could he tell anyone that Ratt had given him hope? Made him see that maybe being different and alone didn't have to be a shameful thing? As silly as it might sound, Boyd wanted to believe that he, too, had a special talent— somewhere, hidden, deep down, ready to emerge.

"Yes," said the librarian softly. "Yes."

"So that's why I want to know. Does he really live

there? Have you ever seen him? Does he look like he does in the pictures?"

Mr. Librarian hopped off the desk and turned his back to Boyd. "You need to accept that there are some things you may never know. Just read the books and don't get greedy. Okay? Do you understand?"

Boyd cleared his throat. "I just want to know—"

"No. Listen. I said, 'Do you understand?' Answer the question." Mr. Librarian spun around and peered into Boyd's face. His long, thin index finger moved back and forth like an upside-down pendulum.

Boyd didn't understand, and he was suddenly afraid. Why was Mr. Librarian being so serious? What if he stopped letting him take the books home? How could anyone's finger move like that? "I understand," he said quickly, clutching *RATT VOLUME 136: THE MARCH OF THE MANNEQUIN'S HAND* to his chest.

"Right," said Mr. Librarian. "Okay." His finger stopped waving. He let out a sigh.

Boyd started for the door. Then stopped. "So you must know him—"

"What did you just promise me?" Finger, finger, finger.

"But he must drop these off—"

"No," said Mr. Librarian sternly, "listen to me. They just show up. I have no dealings with the author." But Boyd could tell, by the look on his face and the tone of his voice—Boyd could tell there was something more.

So Boyd made a promise to himself. Someday he would know the truth about the half man, half rodent who called himself Ratt. Which is why he walked to the library every day during his lunch hour, and then again after school.

Boyd also started watching the house, convinced that behind its sagging walls and boarded-up windows was a clue to the real-life identity of his strange, repulsive, yellow-fanged superhero.

CHAPTER 15

SOPHIE STOPPED AT THE edge of her playground when she saw Tina Louise walking home with me. "We're working on a school project together," I explained.

The three of us walked along in silence for several moments, Sophie sneaking glances at Tina Louise's crotch. "Do you like the monkey bars?" she finally asked, even though, "Did you pee your pants again today?" was what I knew she really wanted to ask.

"I used to like the monkey bars," Tina Louise answered. "Play on them while you can."

Sophie nodded solemnly, even though I knew she had no idea what Tina Louise meant. How can you at seven?

When we reached the front door I said, "Sophie, we'll need some time alone. Work on your jigsaw for fifteen minutes, okay?"

Sophie started to protest, but then Tina Louise said, "Can I see your puzzle?"

Five minutes later, with Sophie completely absorbed in THE HARDEST JIGSAW EVER MADE, Tina Louise and I tiptoed to my room. "You're brilliant," I whispered, closing the door behind us and turning the lock. I grabbed the package from its new hiding place in the closet, then sat down on the floor.

"Here," I said, handing Tina Louise the comic book. I pointed to the hand-drawn picture on the cover. "This is it. The house I told you about."

"Hmmm," she said, shaking her head. "So have you read it?"

"I started to. But it's just this comic about a guy who is half human, half rat. He lives in the house and then this friend from childhood comes to visit him." I opened the book and started to read a few lines out loud. "One night two friends went swimming. It was summer and the moon was full. The two friends hadn't seen each other for a long time. They went swimming from a boat, like they did when they were young."

Tina Louise stopped me there. "Well, your dad. The swimming medal—"

"Yeah. I know," I said. I pulled the medal from inside my shirt. It was warm from being against my skin all day. "So at first I thought it might be related, but honestly, it's just this weird, made-up story. The thing that's most relevant is the picture on the cover. And the word 'drowning.' I keep thinking that maybe it's the place it happened. You know, where he died."

"So there's a swimming medal, a comic book with the house on the cover, and a key to the house—"

"We don't know it's the key to the house."

"It's the key to the house." Tina Louise sat back and tapped the cover of the book with the key. "Here's where your answer is. It's in the house. The book is bait, that's all. Bait for your mom to come looking and she didn't bite. She didn't even nibble."

I nodded slowly. "And I keep wondering about the house. It's our house, but why?"

"If your dad died and the house is suddenly yours, then it's got to be the house he grew up in. This key proves it."

"Maybe," I said, "but it's not like he died yesterday. It's been four years. So why is it ours now?"

"Maybe it's been yours all along. Maybe your mom is just dealing with it now. Her grief, I mean. That's how grief works sometimes." Tina Louise could say things like that. Her mother was a therapist.

"Or maybe not," I said. "Maybe someone else lived there, and maybe he or she died and then left it to my mom. Maybe it's the same person who tried to send her this package."

"Why would your mom send it back without opening it?"

I struggled to come up with an answer. "My mother, well—" I couldn't even finish the sentence. What was I going to say? That my mother was in a coma? That she floated through life like she was in a dream?

"You should ask her, you know."

"I can't. See—my mom, she won't talk."

"Then she should see a therapist."

"She can't stay awake long enough to see a therapist."

Tina Louise was quiet for a moment. Then her face

lit up. "Maybe I could have my mom do an undercover-therapy session on yours. Your mom wouldn't even know what was happening. My mom would be like selling cookies or something and your mom would answer the door—"

"My mom doesn't answer the door."

"Then you would answer the door and ask my mom to come in, and then she'd sit down across from your mom and, whammo, instant therapy."

I thought about it for a moment. Lizzie, drowsy on the couch, one eye on the TV, the other watching Tina Louise's mom suspiciously; Sophie tugging on Tina Louise's mom's sleeve like some hungry pup; me, waiting to hear Lizzie say something revealing, something that would explain all the silence and years of sleep. I shook my head to get rid of the picture. "It wouldn't work," I said.

"Why not?"

"It just wouldn't."

Tina Louise shrugged her shoulders, but I could tell she was disappointed. How could I explain that I didn't know if I even wanted to hear what Lizzie might say? Yes, I wanted to know the answer, but the idea of Lizzie sitting up, putting her feet firmly on the floor and saying, "Okay, here's the truth," well, frankly, it scared me. If silence and sleep were keeping her sane, what would an undercover-therapy session with Tina Louise's mom do to her? Would we have to lock her up? Would she chew off part of her arm like one of those animals caught in an iron-jawed trap?

"I have this feeling," I said slowly, trying to put into words what until then had been wispy, floating images. "I've always had this feeling that there's something different about me. About my family. Especially my dad's side of the family, since my mom won't talk about them at all. And then the house and then, this—" I picked up the comic and flipped through the pages, making the rat man come to life in quick, jerky movements.

When I looked up at Tina Louise her eyes were glowing. She looked ready to explode. "You have to go back there. You have to find out what's in that house. This—" she swept her arm in a wide arc over the package—"this is just the beginning. You have to go there, Margaret."

A tingle began to crawl up my back like a cold, bony finger. What was she saying? Go there without Lizzie? Break into the house?

A loud bang on the door made us both jump. "Margaret!" It was Sophie, pounding on the locked door.

"Hold on, Sophie."

Sophie twisted the knob violently and I could hear her grunt with effort. Tina Louise slapped her hand over her mouth in a motion I now recognized—she was on the verge of the giggles. She climbed onto Sophie's bed and began jumping up and down, her big hair dancing around her laughing face.

"Are you guys jumping on the bed?"

"No," I said.

"I'm telling. I can hear you jumping on the bed."

"Just go away, Sophie."

"I don't have to. It's been fifteen minutes." Sophie scratched on the door for another few seconds, then suddenly, all was silent.

Tina Louise took one last bounce before leaping off the bed and landing in a crouch next to me. "There is a mystery here," she whispered in my ear. "And I know what I'd do if the mystery involved me."

"What?" I whispered back, even though I knew exactly what she was going to say.

She picked up the key and pressed it into my palm, like I'd just won a prize. "It's perfect," she said. "It's Fate."

I looked down at the key. "How do we even know it's to the house?"

"Because it has to be." Tina Louise stood up and grabbed her coat.

"You're leaving?"

"I have to get home. My mom still thinks I can still go into a coma at any moment."

"Can you?"

Tina Louise opened the door to a wide-eyed Sophie holding a screwdriver. "Maybe," she said. "'Bye, Sophie."

"'Bye," said Sophie, suddenly shy.

Very quickly I tucked the medal into my shirt and shoved the comic into the back of my jeans. The key I kept clutched in my sweaty hand.

"Think about it, Margaret," Tina Louise said, half-way out the door. "It's perfect."

"Wait!" I called. She stopped and turned. Something about her seemed bigger and brighter than anything I'd seen before. "Why don't you, you know—" I didn't want Sophie to know what we were talking about.

"What?"

"Come, too," I said.

Tina Louise smiled patiently, at once seeming like a grown-up instead of a kid. "It's your Fate," she said gently. "I have to stay here and suffer the tragic consequences of my own." And with that she raised her arm, gave her Tina Louise salute, and was gone.

I tried to remember her out on the playfield, flat on her back with pee running down her legs, but that already seemed like years ago. Another girl, a different school.

I guided my sister to the bed and told her to sit down. "Sophie," I said, bracing myself for the storm that would follow. "I opened the package."

Sophie sat in stunned silence. Her mouth opened and closed but no words could come out. She ran for my backpack and dumped everything out, then turned to me, her mouth stuck in open position. "Mar-garet!" It came out finally, a half scream, half cry. Like she'd been stabbed.

"Stop it, Sophie," I said.

"Mar-garet!" she cried out again. This time it was followed by a sob. "You lied to me!"

"Come here, Sophie," I said. She shook her head no. Tears were collecting in the corners of her eyes, but she fought to keep them in—too hurt to cry in front of me.

"Here," I said quickly, taking off the swimming medal. "Look at this. It was our dad's."

Sophie stood frozen on the other side of the room, her small arms wrapped tightly around her chest. I went over and knelt down in front of her. "Sophie," I said, placing the blue ribbon around her neck, "it's for you. You can have it."

The tears were too much for her to hold in. They poured from her eyes and made a river down the side of her nose.

"I'm sorry, Sophie," I said. And all at once I was. I really, really was.

"You—let—her—see—it—and—not—me?" She struggled with the words, catching a shaky breath between each one.

"I'm sorry, Sophie," I said again. I held the medal up to her face. "Look, Sophie. Our dad was a champion swimmer. First place."

Sophie shrugged like she didn't care, but I watched her little fingers close gently around the medal.

"And look, here's what's really weird." I reached

around and grabbed the comic from the back of my jeans. "See this book? Look closely. Does anything look familiar?"

Sophie took the book and held it close to her face, but there were still too many tears for her to see it clearly.

"I'm sorry, Sophie," I said again. "If I knew another language I'd say sorry in it, too. I wish I knew a hundred languages. Maybe then I could say it enough so you would forgive me."

Sophie wiped her snotty nose on the back of her hand. "It's okay," she said finally, trying to swallow a sob. She rubbed her eyes and looked at the hand-drawn book. "So is the house our dad's, too?"

"I don't know," I said. "Maybe."

"Can't we ask Mom?"

"No," I said.

"I wish Dad were here, then."

"Me, too," I said.

Sophie snuggled down next to me and leaned in against my shoulder. "Tell me about when he taught you to ride a bike," she said, closing her eyes.

This was Sophie's favorite story about our dad, and she always asked me to tell it when she felt sad. Maybe it was because she didn't have her own memories of him that she treasured mine so much. "Okay," I started, just the way she liked. "I was four when I learned to ride a bike. . . ."

CHAPTER 16

THERE ARE PEOPLE WHO put things in motion and people who become the motion. After a day of planning and two late-night telephone conversations, Tina Louise had somehow put me in motion. *Am I really doing this?* I asked myself Thursday morning as I stepped off the bus and began walking toward the ferry terminal.

The hardest part had been telling Sophie. First she cried, then she pouted, then she threatened to tell Mom if I didn't let her go along. The only thing that had finally calmed her was the promise that if she stayed behind, she could be my mainland link to Tina Louise.

"Teeena Loooo-eeese." Sophie loved to say her name, drawing out every vowel. "Do you call her both names every time?"

"That's her name. Now remember, you have to cover for me with Mom."

"I know," said Sophie. "I'll do the dishes and make the dinner and yell 'STOP IT, MARGARET!' like you're being mean to me."

"Great," I said. "Great, Sophie. I couldn't do this without you."

"What about the Chihuahuas, Margaret?" My little sister started to chew on her fingers.

"You'll be fine," I said.

"But what if there's an earthquake?"

"I'm not going that far, Sophie. I'll only be gone a day, maybe two. It's just a ferry ride away."

"It was a long drive."

"Not that long."

"So you'll be back tomorrow?"

"Probably. I hope so, Sophie."

"Will you promise?"

"I can't, Sophie. I don't know what I'm going to find or how long it will take to find it. But this is important. Don't you want to know what's in the house? Don't you want to know the mystery of our dad?"

Sophie fingered the swimming medal which hadn't left her neck since I'd put it on her. "Yes," she said finally. "Yes I do."

There was a time, before my mom got so sleepy, that we rode the ferry often. It was right after my dad died and Lizzie suddenly got this huge burst of energy—like she'd somehow been zapped with the combined superpower of both a mom and a dad. It lasted about two years.

She got promoted three times at work. She took a gourmet cooking class. While we ate by the light of hand-dipped candles made in her craft group, she would explain how cameras worked and how an initiative became a law. And, like I said, we rode the ferry often.

I loved riding the ferry. The ferry workers all

smiled and the food was delicious. While Lizzie looked for an empty booth next to a window, Sophie and I would run to the cafe to order our food. Then we'd wander around the ferry looking for her, our paper plates piled high with steaming-hot fries. We'd only sit long enough to finish half of the fries—the rest we'd take outside, onto the deck.

With the wind in our hair and the salty spray on our faces, we'd hold a fry up over our heads. Within seconds a seagull would appear, hovering over us and squawking loudly. Then, at just the right moment, he'd swoop down and pluck the french fry from between our fingers. No matter how many times we did this, it always made us laugh.

Then, like I said, everything changed. I think my mother used up her life's worth of allotted energy in just a couple of years. She was like a wind-up toy that simply wound down and had no one around to crank her back up. Sophie and I tried for a while, but then we got used to the new way of things. I didn't miss the fancy food, really. Or the political discussions or the handmade candles. I did miss the ferry rides. I missed the islands. So Thursday morning, when I bought my ticket and walked up the passenger plank to the ferry, I didn't feel scared or alone or anything. I felt at home. Right at home.

The first thing I did was head straight to the cafe for a plate of those fries. Time didn't matter on the ferry—you could eat fries for breakfast and a donut for dinner. Next I found an empty booth right next to a window and tossed my backpack on the seat. I sat down and rested my head against the cold window. The sun was soft and sleepy and the ferry was quiet and nearly empty—a handful of men and women in business suits reading the paper and breathing into steaming cups of coffee, a few moms holding round, drowsy babies, a janitor sweeping the floor.

"Remember to breathe," Tina Louise had told me on the phone the night before. Apparently, it's something her therapist mother prescribed to all her patients.

I took a deep breath and closed my eyes, then kept them closed as the ferry whistle blew once, twice. I felt a small jolt as the ferry dislodged from the dock, and then I was just floating, moving with the boat. *Breathe*, I told myself. *Breathe*. When I finally opened my eyes there was no land in sight. Even if I'd wanted to, there was no way I could turn back now. I looked down at my plate of fries and suddenly felt too queasy to eat them.

"The key," Tina Louise had also whispered into the phone, "is not to think too far ahead. For example, get yourself on the ferry and look at the water. Don't think of anything but the water. Got it?"

"Got it," I said.

"When the ferry docks on the other side, walk off with the other passengers."

"Right," I said.

"When you hit the main road, start walking."

"Walking."

"Think about the plan," she said.

"The plan."

"Remember—if you believe it, it will happen."

Believe it. It had sounded so simple, so right the night before. Concentrate on the water, my french fries, a seagull hovering over my outstretched hand. Think about anything but what comes next. The aloneness of the trip and the huge old house and that flicker of movement in the upstairs window—the thing you've been telling yourself was just a reflection of the sun.

The ferry horn must have blasted our arrival to shore. I must have stood up. I must have thrown away my untouched plate of soggy fries. I must have walked with the other passengers to the lower deck and waited as the ferry workers hooked the boat to the dock. It's just that I don't remember any of that. Suddenly I was standing on firm ground and feeling completely alone—more alone than I'd ever felt at school, even when I was eating my lunch in the bathroom stall.

It would have been so easy to turn around, step back on the ferry and ride it home. But then I remembered the last thing Tina Louise had said to me. It was on the phone the night before. I was sitting in my pajamas in the dark. "Your life will never change—"

"Why?" I asked.

"You didn't let me finish. I was going to say—your life will never change until you take the first step."

The first step.

Tina Louise was right. I turned away from the ferry dock and the friendly workers and the best fries in the state of Washington and I took the first step.

CHAPTER 17

TINA LOUISE HAD SAID that it was very important to look like I knew what I was doing at all times—otherwise someone might ask me who I was or where I was going. "You just don't know who you can trust," she'd said.

I stopped at the intersection where Lizzie had stopped just a few days earlier and followed the arrow to town. When I reached Main Street, I felt comforted by the signs of everyday, normal life. There was the touristy shop with the pink-shelled hula girls. There was the post office and the darkened tavern. The bright yellow library. The drugstore. As I glanced in the drugstore window, I suddenly wanted to step inside.

The drugstore was the kind of place you'd see in a movie. Its shelves were stocked with one of everything: one deck of cards, one pocketknife, one squirt gun, one dog leash. It even had an old-fashioned food counter right in the middle where a redheaded waitress stood watching me, a pot of coffee in one hand, a bleached washrag in the other.

I nodded my hello, then wandered around the aisles. My backpack was already full of provisions for survival—sandwiches and candles, matches, and a flashlight with extra batteries. But since I needed directions to Waterfront Road, I thought I might as well get a candy bar while I was at it.

As I passed the row of cereal, I thought about Sophie. "I hope she made it to school on time," I said to myself. "I hope she ate her breakfast and brushed her teeth." *I hope she isn't as scared as I am.*

I grabbed a handful of candy bars. Then, even though I didn't need them, went back for the corn-flakes. I hugged the box to my chest and looked around for the cash register.

"You can pay for that here, hon," said the waitress. I walked over to the food counter. The smell of grease and meat was making me hungry and queasy at the same time. An old man sat at the counter eating a hamburger. He took a bite, then gently patted his mouth with a paper napkin, the way some women do after putting on lipstick.

Without glancing his way, I set my things on the counter.

"Good milk shakes," said the old man, slurping down the last of his.

"Good," I said finally, glancing over at him. His flannel shirt was neatly pressed and buttoned all the way to the top of his neck.

"Okay, hon," said the waitress, "you owe me three dollars and seventy-nine cents."

I put a twenty on the counter, trying not to feel guilty that I'd taken it from my mother's purse the night before.

"Good donuts, too," said the old man. "They make them right here."

The waitress counted back my change and I shoved it in my pocket. "You want something to eat?" she asked.

"How much are the donuts?"

"Fifty cents."

"I'll have a donut," I said.

"Freshly made and cherry filled," said the old man. "Best kept secret on the island. Must be a school holiday today."

"No, it's not," said the waitress with a wink. She put a donut on a plate and set it on the counter in front of me. "I put my kids on the bus this morning."

"I'm just visiting," I said. I took a bite of donut. It was soft and chewy with just the perfect amount of sweet icing and cherry filling.

"I thought so," said the old man. "Never seen you before. Kids can change, though. So fast. Fluffy bunnies one day and then, wham. Not anymore. More like wild boars. Where are you from, then?"

I motioned to my mouth full of donut and chewed vigorously, all the while trying to imagine how a wild boar might make it to an island.

"Chew it up good," said the old man. "Don't want to be doing no CPR this early in the day. Can't say I believe in that stuff anyway."

My hands were sweating. I chewed, I swallowed. "I'm meeting a friend," I said. "On Waterfront Road.

She said it was easy to get to from town—"

The waitress nodded. "Go out, take a left and follow Main until you can't go any farther."

"You'll come to a T," the old man added. "Take a left at the T and you'll end up on Waterfront Road. A right takes you to the school."

I looked at the clock. If I was home right now, I'd be eating my lunch in a bathroom stall. I finished the rest of the donut in three bites and put fifty cents on the counter. Then I remembered about the tip and put down two more dimes.

"Thanks, hon," said the waitress. "Good luck to you."

"Thanks," I said back, not yet realizing how much I'd need it. I stuffed the cornflakes and candy bars into my backpack and headed for the door. On my way out I heard the old man ask the waitress, "Where'd she say she was from?"

III

CHAPTER 18

"YOU'D BETTER GET GOING," said Mr. Librarian.

Boyd glanced at the clock on the wall and jumped. He had seven minutes before lunch was officially over—and a ten-minute walk back to school. He put the comic back on the shelf then grabbed the newest volume. "Good-bye, Mr. Librarian," he called, waving the book in the air as he headed for the door. "See you after school."

"I'll be here," Mr. Librarian murmured, barely glancing up from his piles of old newspapers and stacks of scrapbooks.

Boyd stepped out into the sunshine, glanced down at his watch and started to run. *Smack!* Suddenly he was on the ground with the wind knocked out of him. He looked up, expecting to see a wall or a truck or a very large man, but instead found himself looking into the startled gray eyes of a girl about his age. She wasn't a girl he recognized from school, but something about her seemed familiar.

"Sorry," she said, holding out her hand to help him up. "I wasn't looking where I was going."

Flustered, Boyd turned away from her hand and scrambled awkwardly to his feet. "It's okay," he said, "I wasn't looking, either." He glanced at her again, but she was no longer looking at his face; she was looking past him with an expression he couldn't quite make out. Boyd turned to see what had caught her attention—and there on the ground was his latest Ratt book.

Feeling the blood rush to his cheeks, Boyd grabbed the book from the ground and shoved it into his backpack. Even the kids who didn't tease him outright about his books laughed at him behind his back.

"What was that?" she asked, nodding at his backpack.

Boyd pretended to not understand. "It's a backpack."

"No, the book. The comic book."

"Well, then. You just answered your own question. It's a comic book."

The girl narrowed her eyes like she was ready to say something else, but Boyd wasn't about to stand there and let her make fun of him. Swinging his backpack over his shoulder, he took off running—down Main Street, toward the T.

CHAPTER 19

THAT BOY! THE BOOK! The drawing on the cover! I watched him run down the street, arms and legs flying. Should I run after him? He was probably heading to school. But if I actually caught up with him, what would I do then? Show him my book? Tell him about my dad and the house and the package I found there?

Trust no one, Tina Louise whispered in my ear. *No one.* I turned to the bright yellow building where the boy had just been. The sign on the door said LIBRARY. Was this Fate? Was this how it worked? I took a deep breath and opened the door.

A jingly bell announced my arrival. I looked around the dimly lit room—a complete contrast to the cheery yellow on the outside. Was anyone even there?

"Yes?" a voice said from the corner.

I turned in the direction and spotted a skinny little man at a large wooden desk, nearly hidden behind a tall stack of newspapers, magazines, and loose-leaf notebooks. He stared at me like I'd stepped into his living room without knocking first. His mustache twitched and he repeated, "Yes?"

"Um, is this the library?" I asked. The air in the room was stuffy and stale.

"Does it look like a library?"

I glanced around. There were shelves and there

were books. "Yes," I said.

"Okay, then." The man turned back to the news-paper. A long pair of scissors gleamed in his hand.

"I, um, am looking for a book—" I started.

"Yes." Clip, clip. "So I assumed."

I took a step closer. The man glared. I froze. "Well, do you have a computer—or, like a card file or some-thing?"

"We don't work like that. It's all up here." He tapped his head with the sharp point of the scissors.

"Okay," I said. "Then I guess I'll just look around." I started toward the closest aisle.

"We're alphabetical by subject," he called out over the *clip, clip* of the scissors. "Unless you're looking for poetry, that's under P."

I pulled out a book from the middle of the shelf. *Aquariums in Restaurant Lobbies*, by Mr. Andrew Andrews.

"You're in Aquariums," called out the librarian.

"Yes," I called back. I flipped open the book to a carefully drawn picture of a small, tropical fish. Under-neath were the words, "This is Buddy. He's in the lobby of Shanghai Garden in Bremerton, Washington. I've watched him for two years, now, and I've been told he's eaten every new batch of offspring that has ever been born."

I put the book down and pulled out another—a handwritten journal of baby Anna's first year. This was like no library I'd ever seen before.

"Finding everything okay?" I jumped. The librarian was suddenly right at my side, scratching his nose with the sharp end of a pair of scissors. The name on his name tag said MR. LIBRARIAN. "Finding what you need?" he asked again.

"Actually, no. I'm looking for real information." I said it as politely as I could, but the librarian scowled.

"Buddy kills his offspring—you don't think that's real?"

"I mean, I'm looking for specific information about a house. I have a book with a house on the cover and I just saw a boy with a book that looked almost exactly the same—" I stopped. Trust no one. Had I already given away too much? "So you don't have like old newspapers or files on things that happened on this island?"

"No."

I glanced back at his desk and the pile of yellowed newspapers. "You don't?"

He pretended not to notice the direction of my stare. "You said you had a book. A book with an old mansion on the cover?"

"No I didn't."

We eyed each other suspiciously. Finally his mustache did a nervous little dance. He turned away.

I followed him back to his desk. "So," I pressed, "you don't have information on things like people who died and how they died and things like that?"

He settled back into his seat and picked up another

yellowed newspaper. Licked his index finger like grown-ups do and made a grand gesture of flipping over the first page. "Not for public use."

I watched him scan the newspaper, then pierce the center of it with his scissors. I cleared my throat. "I don't mean this as rude or anything, but is this a real library?"

The librarian didn't look up. "It's a library," he answered coldly. "But it's unique. One of a kind. Nothing like it. Except two that I know of for sure. Maybe more."

"What do you mean?"

He sighed and lowered the paper to where I could see his face. Then he rested his elbows on the desk and eyed me wearily, like he'd been through this a thousand times before. "People write their stories and bring them in. I put them in order and know where they are."

"You mean anyone can just come in and give you something they wrote?"

"Yes."

"So nothing here is actually published?"

"We don't accept published works. Too mainstream."

"Well, if I'm looking for information on a house—"

"Which house?"

"The big one on Waterfront Road," I said.

The librarian narrowed his eyes. Then, without a word he pushed himself away from his desk, stood up and whisked past me to a far side of the library. I hesitated, then followed.

"Here," he said, handing me a book. Even before I looked down, I knew what it was.

"But this," I said, "this is a comic book."

"It's all I have on that particular house. Do you want it or not?"

I nodded slowly.

"Do you have a library card?" he asked, knowing perfectly well that I didn't.

"No," I said.

"Then you can't check one out."

"What do I need for a library card?"

"Your name, for starters. And an address and telephone number."

"I'll just read it here." The entire shelf was bursting with more just like it, and there was a small stool for sitting.

With a curt nod the librarian walked back to his desk and left me alone in the Rs. *What was I doing here?* I pulled out a comic and flipped open the cover. The Ratt man was sniffing through a garbage can. I sighed.

"Although this is not a conventional library," Mr. Librarian called out, "you might be surprised at what you find. Maybe more than a factie-packed microfiche, computerated establishment might even think to offer. People tell their stories in all sorts of ways. You just need to know how to look." Then he started to hum.

I peeked at him through a crack in the book-shelves—a strange little man clipping and pasting and clipping and pasting. He gave a sigh, slapped a book shut, and added it to a stack of others on his desk.

"What are those?" I called out.

He jumped like he'd forgotten I was there. "Stories from years past—" he started to answer, then glanced at the stack of yellowed newspapers at his elbow and pursed his lips together.

Hmmm. Exactly what I had just asked for. "Can I see one?"

"No," he said. "They're mine. A work in progress."

I glanced at the shelf above his head—it was crammed with books just like the ones on his desk. When I squinted I could make out some of the hand-written titles: SPORTS, MARRIAGES, DIVORCE, STORMS, MURDER, BIRTHS, DEATHS, VARIOUS. I looked down at the book in my hand—the Ratt man was running from some kids in an alley. There were no answers here.

I stood up. "Thanks for your help. I'm leaving now."

"Come again," Mr. Librarian cried cheerily, his sharp eyes following me all the way to the door.

Outside the sun was still bright and high in the sky, but when I thought about the shelf full of comic books, the old abandoned mansion, and the long walk ahead of me, I felt chilled to the bone.

CHAPTER 20

WHEN I WAS LITTLE, right after my dad died, I started having bad dreams. The worst was the Green Fizzy-Water Dream. In this dream, Sophie, Mom, Dad, and I were having a picnic in the woods. We found a beautiful green rock next to a deep river and decided to sit on it. Dad went first, but the minute he sat on the rock, he slid down into the water. Mom stepped onto the rock to grab him, but she slipped into the water, too. Then Sophie and I ran after them both and, even though we tried our best to hang on, the rock was just too slippery. Suddenly we, too, were sinking into the deep, green fizzy water.

I'd wake up from this dream and run to my mother's bedroom. "Tell me your dream," she'd say, moving over so I could climb in next to her. "It's not as scary if you say it out loud." So I would tell her about the picnic and the slippery rock and the green fizzy water that stung our skin. And how we could see each other under the water, but couldn't help each other. And then she would say, "Okay, now finish it in a happy way."

I'd close my eyes and go back to the place underwater. And I would open my mouth and take in a little gulp and realize that it was really just sweet, fizzy soda pop. And then I'd drink it and drink it and Sophie and

Mom and Dad would see me drinking it, so they'd start drinking it and we'd all drink it until it was gone. And then, our stomachs full and burpy, we'd stand up and walk down the dry riverbed, laughing because we were so smart and lucky and happy.

I hadn't remembered the dream or Lizzie's Happy-Ending game until that lonely walk along Waterfront Road. Occasionally a car would whiz past and I'd watch it from the cover of a tree, but other than that I felt like I was the only person left on the planet. Late in the afternoon, a yellow school bus lumbered by, making me think about everything back home. Sophie and Tina Louise, and my mother coming home from work, kicking off her shoes and lying down for a nap on the couch. Already I felt I'd been gone a long, long time.

By about five, when the sun had moved so low it could no longer find its way through the thick branches of the trees, I started to worry. How much farther was the water? And when I made it to the water, how long would it take me to reach the house?

And, of course, there were the noises—noises that had been with me all day long, but now seemed to have gotten louder, more steady, not so much like falling pinecones or scurrying mice anymore. So, with every new rustle in the woods, I forced myself to play Lizzie's game.

"Here," I say to the leader of the wild boars. *"Have some cornflakes."*

"Hmm. This is good. We've never had cereal

before—just human flesh. Thank you. You are now our friend. "

It was a lot of work, coming up with a happy ending for each noise in the woods, and just when I thought I'd used them all up, the trees parted and there it was—that pure blue expanse of water.

I felt elated, but only for a second. I'd made it this far, but how much longer did I have to go? I thought back to the drive. How many times had Sophie bounced up and down? How many fingernails had Lizzie bitten off?

Just keep walking, I said to myself. That's all I could do. Step, step. I watched the sun sparkle on the water, easing itself down to what looked like the edge of the world. Would I make it to the house before it slipped completely out of sight? Or would I be walking on a strange road, all alone, in the dark? I glanced at my watch. If I was home right now, I'd be eating a bean burrito.

I walked until my blisters rubbed away to raw skin. The sun had already made its big, beautiful, pink and orange exit, but I wasn't completely in the dark, thanks to the bright and nearly full moon. Still, my fingers were nervous as they fished the flashlight from my backpack.

And that's when I saw it—up ahead, what looked like a porch light. I was confused at first. Would my old, abandoned mansion have a porch light? No. But then I remembered—the little beige house next door would.

That had to be it.

Elated, I reached down into my pocket and felt around for the key. Not there. The other pocket? Not there, either. Where was it? My backpack? I swung my backpack around and fumbled with the zipper. And then I heard it. A noise across the road, a slow and steady noise. Deliberate, like footsteps. And getting closer. *Crunch, crunch, crunch.*

Get inside, I heard the wind whisper. Even though I hadn't found the key, I pulled the backpack to my chest and started to run. *Crunch-crunch-crunch.* The noise across the road seemed to match my new pace.

I ran faster, keeping my eyes locked on the light. Happy ending. *I reach the house and my mother is waiting for me. No, my father. And he holds out his hand and says, "I hope my very noisy puppy didn't scare you back there."*

My feet hit gravel. I stumbled, but didn't fall. *The gravel drive?* I realized I still had the flashlight in my hand. I turned it on and swung it around. *Yes, it was the gravel drive—and there were the dark hedges, standing like guards over the house. I'd made it!*

I don't remember running through the overgrown yard, or up the creaking steps. But somehow I was standing on the front porch, digging through my backpack for the key. Cornflakes, candy bars, sandwiches, candles, sweatshirt, an extra pair of jeans, socks—

but where was the key? Finally, at the very bottom of the pack, my fingers curled around something small and hard. I pulled it out. *Crunch-CRUNCH, Crunch-CRUNCH.* It was the key!

One shaking hand held the flashlight while the other reached out to fit the key into the rusted lock. Was it even the right key? Tina Louise had been so sure. *Crunch-CRUNCH.*

How can I begin to explain what happened next? Even now, it's such a blur to me. I know what happened first. What happened first was, I dropped the key.

I DROPPED THE KEY.

And as I got on my hands and knees, pawing desperately at the ground, the noise continued to move closer. *Crunch-CRUNCH.*

Don't panic, I told my fluttering hands as they moved across the rough wood. *Pat, pat, pat.*

Wait—the flashlight. As soon as I remembered I swung the flashlight around the porch, but its small circle of light barely made a dent in the darkness. My hands started in blindly again on the porch floor. *Pat, pat, pat. Pat, pat, pat. Clink.*

There it was. The clink of metal on wood. My trembling fingers grabbed it and held on tight. *Now, take the key, shove it in the lock. Turn, turn, turn.* I did that. I did what I was supposed to do. But the door didn't open.

Crunch, crunch. Now there was no mistaking the

noise. Those were footsteps behind me. Two-footed footsteps meant not a Chihuahua, not a wild boar. *Crunch. Crunch.* They meant something that walked upright.

Please, please, please, I whispered to the door, the lock, my own trembling hands. *Please work together. Please fit. Please save me from whatever is on two feet and closing in quickly.*

I turned the key the other way. This time I felt the bolt start to move and then heard a click—the door was unlocked! I turned the knob and pushed, but still nothing happened.

I held the knob with one hand, turned my body and slammed my shoulder against the door. Nothing.

I slammed it again.

This time the door gave up. With a creak and a groan, the old hinges swung open and I tumbled inside.

Close the door, close the door. The sound was still out there and the door was wide open. I stood up, pushed it shut and reached for the bolt. I twisted and turned. *Is it locked?* I tried the knob and it didn't move. It was locked. I was safe.

I slid to the floor and put my head between my knees, just like Mrs. P.E. told us to do when we were about to faint. *Breathe,* I told myself. *You can breathe now.*

I heard my own loud and shaking breath in the room—and nothing else. Whatever was out there was out there. If it tried to get in I would hear it first. I was in and that meant safe.

The moon had managed to find its way through slits in the boarded-up windows, lighting a huge living room with what appeared to be long couches, over-stuffed chairs, end tables and lamps—all completely covered in heavy white sheets. It was a room frozen and waiting.

Very slowly, I shone the flashlight in the dark corners of the room. Nothing moved or jumped or snarled. I looked down at the key in my hand, then shoved it deep into the front pocket of my jeans. My fingers were still trembling.

With the moon lighting the room in its sweet, gentle way, I sat perfectly still and told myself that this was my home, and that nothing could hurt me now. That was my couch, my fireplace, my chair. There would be plenty of time to find out what was beyond this room; right then all I wanted to do was sit, rest, and pretend I was safe at home.

CHAPTER 21

"DAD!" FOR THE SECOND TIME in less than five minutes, Boyd ran out to the living room where his father was watching a cooking show on TV. ("I've given up meat, son, but I don't have to give up the sight and sounds of it," is how he'd explained his nightly habit.)

"Dad, the light in the old house—I saw it again! First on the porch and now there's someone inside!" He grabbed his father's arm and tugged.

"Give me a minute, Boyd. They're stuffing the chicken with garlic and rosemary. They're just about to roast it."

"No, Dad. You have to come *now!*"

Boyd's father stood up heavily and followed his son down the hallway. By the time he stepped past the BOYD'S ROOM sign on the door, Boyd was already back at his window, eyes fixed on the old mansion. "Okay, Dad. Just watch. Just wait."

And so he did. He watched. He waited. Then he cleared his throat the way dads do.

"Dad, I swear it," Boyd said.

Boyd's dad patted him on the shoulder. "I think maybe you've been reading too many stories about that place, son. I'm going back to my chicken. Call if you need me." Boyd heard his father leave the room, but he stayed at the window, waiting.

CHAPTER 22

I STOOD AT THE BOTTOM of the huge staircase and tried to convince myself that I should wait until morning. I'd already examined every corner of the living room—flung every sheet off the heavy old furniture and shone my flashlight up and down all the cracks in the walls. The other rooms on the first floor—the kitchen, dining room, library, and den—were like storage rooms, so crammed full of crates and cardboard boxes that I couldn't step more than a foot inside.

If I waited until morning it would be light. If I waited until morning I could move more quickly. I thought about Sophie back home in the corner of the living room, working on her jigsaw puzzle all alone. I thought about my mother and the secret she'd been keeping from us all these years. How could I wait until morning?

Creak. I heard my foot on the first step. It made a sound that echoed through the house. *Creak.* Second step, too. *Cre-eak.* Was that my foot? Or did it come from upstairs? I stopped and held my breath. Nothing. I took another step. *Cre-eak.* And another. *Don't think, just move.* Halfway to the top was another landing, and then the stairway twisted sharply to the left. I stopped on the landing and pointed the flashlight up, but couldn't see past my outstretched hand.

So I took another step. And another. And somehow, without really wanting to be, I found myself at the top of the stairs. The air seemed chillier on the second floor, and damp, too. Plus, without any windows, it was pitch black—almost like stepping into a cave.

I ran the flashlight along the sides of the wide hallway. Four big, heavy doors—two on the left and two on the right—and all of them shut. *This is silly*, I said to myself. *Go downstairs and wait for morning.* But even as I said it, I knew I wouldn't. It wasn't some test of bravery or even curiosity anymore. It was just that if I turned around and went downstairs, it would mean there was something to be afraid of. And if there was something to be afraid of, then how would I be able to spend the rest of the night in that house, even downstairs where the moon made it nice and cozy? And if I couldn't spend the night in the house, then what would I do? Walk out the door and back through the woods to the ferry terminal? I had to keep going forward simply because if I didn't, I'd have to go back. And that would be even worse.

I decided to open every door. I wouldn't go in all the way—just open the door, shine the flashlight long enough to convince myself there was nothing to be afraid of, then move on to the next.

In front of the first door I paused and took a deep breath. *Could this have been my father's room?* As I pushed it open, a waft of cold air hit me, much colder than the air in the hallway. But the room itself was surprisingly well lit, thanks to big bay windows and the moon. I lowered the flashlight and stepped inside.

How can I describe what was in that room? You know the one drawer in the house that doesn't make sense? Some people call it the junk drawer, but it's not full of junk, really—just full of things that don't have a place of their own. That's what this was, only a hundred times bigger with a hundred times more stuff, like the back porch where I'd discovered the package, only with many many things. Stacks of old newspapers and balls of twine, bottle caps and piles of tinfoil, pencil stubs, cigarette lighters, books without covers and covers without books, pretty candy wrappers and deflated balloons, matchbooks and maps from all over the world, polished rocks and cement blocks, a row of antique sewing machines and a pile of frayed patchwork quilts, basketballs, baseballs, footballs, and a hockey puck, a three-seated bicycle with no handlebars, a bright yellow YIELD FOR PEDESTRIANS sign, a dollhouse, at least a hundred dolls (most without heads), a suitcase of full of glittery dresses.

Here, think of something right now. A pogo stick? That was in the room. A rubber ball? That was in the room. A giant deer lawn ornament? That was, too. Anything you could think of, it was in the room. And maybe it was just the way the moonlight shone on the metal and tin, but it all looked so pretty. Sophie would love this room, I thought to myself as I backed out into the hallway. She would want to stay and touch every single thing in it.

I left the door open for the little bit of moonlight that could reach to the hallway, then I stood in front of door number two. Feeling a little more confident, I reached out and took the knob in my hand.

If the first room was a junk drawer, this one was a workbench—a giant workbench. Long, heavy wooden tables lined each wall of this room. I shone my flashlight above the tables and saw tools—hundreds of tools all hanging from little metal hooks. Big tools, tiny tools, some I recognized, most I did not.

Cre-eak. I froze. Did that sound come from me? I waited for another, but heard nothing. It must have been my feet on the old wooden floorboards, I told myself. Just old floorboards settling—and only two more doors to go. Then I could go downstairs and maybe even sleep. I stepped back into the hallway, once again leaving the door open.

When I opened the door to the third room the first thing I noticed was the heavy, warm smell of paint. Paint, paint thinner, ink—all familiar from junior high art classes. As I shone my flashlight around, I began to get a funny tingle in my stomach. There was something wrong about this room, but I couldn't quite put my finger on what it was. It seemed to be some sort of artist's studio, complete with boxes of pencil stubs and brushes, stacks of mismatched paper, and a giant paper cutter that looked a lot like an old-fashioned guillotine.

I shifted my backpack to my other shoulder and pointed the flashlight at one of the many easels lined up on the far side of the room. I could make out a few shapes, but nothing more. As I moved a little closer, the shapes took on familiar angles. A peaked roof, battered shingles, a broken window—it was the mansion. My mansion.

It was at that moment I realized what had been making my stomach feel funny. It was the smell of paint. Not dried up and long-ago abandoned paint, but wet paint. *Fresh paint.*

Cre-eak.

This time I didn't wonder—I knew. That sound wasn't coming from me or from an old house settling into the ground. There was someone else in the house. I turned off the flashlight, crouched down and ordered myself to stay calm. Very slowly, I inched my way toward the door. Every muscle in my body was begging to jump up and run, but I held back, thinking that if I moved slowly, I could sneak out of the room and down the stairs undetected.

I think your body sometimes knows things before your brain does—that's how it felt anyway. My heart started beating too fast for my slow-moving body. *Run, run, run,* it seemed to shout. *What are you waiting for? RUN!*

But I didn't run—not yet. I scrunched up, trying to make myself as small as I could be. I thought about Sophie—how when we were little we used to play hide-and-seek and, whenever I was it, Sophie would stand in the middle of the room and close her eyes. She'd stand there with a silly grin on her face and her eyes closed, believing that if she couldn't see me, then I couldn't see her.

I used to think that was so funny, but you know what? Scrunched up like a potato bug and light-headed from paint fumes, I was doing the exact same thing.

"Open your eyes, Margaret." Tina Louise was suddenly next to me, whispering in my ear. "You can't move with your eyes closed."

I opened my eyes. I looked toward the door. And that's when I saw it. A large, hulking shadow gliding silently past the doorway.

I didn't wait anymore. I jumped up. Would it grab me if I made a dash for the door? Maybe, but it was my only chance, my only way out.

So, heart bursting and body trembling, I ran. I ran out the door and down the wide hallway, past dark corners and shadows that seemed to have suddenly sprung to life.

At the end of the hallway I heard a strange sound, like a growl, and then felt something brush against my leg. Without thinking, I flung my backpack in its direction and stumbled down the first few steps. As I reached out for the banister the flashlight slipped from my hand, bumping and banging all the way to the bottom of the stairs. I was now in the darkest part of the house, without my flashlight, completely blind.

Get out, the house creaked and the shadows hissed, *out out out*. I let the banister lead me down the winding staircase. How much farther? I remember thinking the words just as my feet tripped over the bottom step. I felt for the wall, then let it lead me to the living room. There was the moon, just where I'd left it, lighting the way to the front door.

Cre-eak. Something was still growling around my legs, but it was the memory of the hulking figure that kept me running. Straight for the door, without looking back.

CHAPTER 23

BOYD STOOD OUTSIDE ON the lawn, waiting for another flash of light to appear in one of the upstairs windows. Had he really seen them at all? Or had his father been right?

Trust your instincts, Ratt would say in a situation like this. *Your instincts are never wrong.*

So Boyd stood firm and waited for an instinct to come and tell him what to do. And just then the door to the mansion flew open and a ghostly figure leaped onto the porch.

A ghostly figure? No, it wasn't. Boyd blinked and looked again. It was just a girl.

He watched the girl hesitate on the front porch. She glanced out across the road and to the edge of the dark forest. As her face turned into the moonlight, Boyd took a step forward. Yes it was—it was her. "Hey," he called out.

The girl jumped, looked behind her, then flew down the porch steps, across the yard and to the other side of the road. At the edge of the forest she hesitated, then quickly slipped into the dark forest.

Boyd watched the spot on the edge of the road where the girl had disappeared. He waited again for instinct to tell him what to do. "Come on," he urged.

"What?" Instinct asked.

"I need you to tell me what to do. That's what instincts are for."

"Okay."

"Okay what?"

"Okay," Instinct said finally, softly, weakly. "Run?"

"Really?" Boyd asked, giving it a chance to change its mind.

"Well, yeah," Instinct said, cringing. "Run, Boyd, run. I guess."

CHAPTER 24

I RAN. THIS IS HOW I'd imagined running from a swarm of killer bees. A pack of wild Chihuahuas. I ran so fast that, for once, Mrs. P.E. would have been proud. And I would have gotten a lot farther, too, if it hadn't been for the tree root that caught hold of my ankle. As I fell, clumps of dirt and moss and dead leaves filled my mouth. Dazed, I sat up and listened for the crashing of footsteps.

Yes—they were still there. And moving closer.

Staying low to the ground I pulled myself behind the nearest tree. The moon had managed to find an opening in the thick cover of branches and was now turned on me like a spotlight. I scrunched my body into a tight ball and waited. The footsteps stopped.

"Hello?" It was a voice—one not coming from my own head.

I opened my eyes. I hadn't known they were closed. In front of me stood a boy. He was about my size, but that's all I could see in the darkness.

"I'm not chasing you," he said.

"Who are you chasing?"

"I was following you."

"Oh," I said. I stood up slowly and brushed the dirt from my jacket.

"See, I just live next door and I saw a light in the

mansion. So I watched it, waiting for him. But you ran out."

I took a step closer to get a better look at his face. "You're the boy from town," I said, feeling a chill when I recognized him. "The boy with the comic book."

"Yes," he said softly. "Strange, huh?"

"Yes," I said, "strange." The comic book, the house on the cover—something had brought us together twice in one day. It was the most amazing, spooky, strange, and wonderful thing that could have happened. Fate, Tina Louise?

"I'm Boyd," he said, offering his hand the way a grown-up man might do.

"I'm Margaret," I said, taking his hand and shaking it solemnly. It was not so much a handshake as an offering, a pact.

The boy looked around, as if slowly surfacing from some disturbing dream. He glanced at the moon through the tree branches and said, "Let's get out of here."

"Okay," I said and waited for him to lead. When he didn't, I asked, "Which way?"

"My instinct says—" and he paused, tilting his head to one side. Then he shrugged and said, "I don't know. Let's just start walking."

"So tell me, what were you doing in the house?"

We'd been stumbling through the dark forest for several minutes when he asked it. What could I say?

How much could I tell? Instead of answering, I asked him a question back. "You said you were watching the house for him. Who is him?"

"You mean you don't know? You weren't looking for him, too?"

"Who?" I asked. I kept thinking of the handshake. For a moment, when his fingers first brushed against mine, I'd felt dizzy. The handshake meant this: Trust me and I'll trust you. Besides Tina Louise, I hadn't trusted another kid in a long time. "Who?" I asked again.

"Well," he said finally. "Well. I was watching the house for Ratt."

I couldn't help myself. I started to laugh.

CHAPTER 25

BOYD FELT HER LAUGHTER in his gut, his chest, every finger and every toe. He felt it burn his throat and his cheeks and the back of his neck, too. Trust no one was the Ratt's motto, and Boyd had lived by it, too—until tonight. Tonight he'd been tricked by a girl because she was pretty and seemed nice and had taken his hand when he'd held it out. Well, she wasn't nice, Boyd decided, and she could just find her own way out of the woods.

He picked up his pace, trying to break away from her.

"I'm sorry," she said, stumbling through the over-growth but managing to keep up.

Boyd walked faster.

"I'm really sorry," she said again.

Boyd started to run. He heard her struggling after him and he smiled to himself—just see her try and make it out of these woods alone. The next moment he was flat on his face, his feet tangled in blackberry vines. *I think I will lie here and pretend to be dead,* he said to himself. He couldn't really think of anything else to do.

CHAPTER 26

"ARE YOU OKAY?" I knelt down next to Boyd and touched his shoulder.

He didn't move.

"Boyd?" I said. "Boyd, are you okay?" I shook him gently, but still he didn't move. What if he was really hurt? What if he'd landed on a rock and had crushed his skull? What if he was in a coma?

"Boyd, I'll go for help. I'll go and—get your mom." I stood up, ready to run. My heart was pounding.

"I'm okay." Boyd sat up quickly but didn't look at me. Carefully he began to untangle his ankles from the clinging blackberry vines.

Awkwardly I stood and watched, knowing he didn't want my help. "I'm sorry," I said softly. "I'm sorry I laughed."

As soon as he got one foot free he started in on the other.

"I don't know why I laughed. I know about the Ratt man, too—"

"He's not the Ratt man."

"What?"

"He's Ratt. Just Ratt."

"Okay," I said. "Anyway, I was going to tell you why I was in the house."

"I don't care anymore." He untangled the other

foot and stood up slowly. "Let's just get out of here."

We walked along in silence. Was there anything I could say that would get back the feeling of the handshake? "Listen," I tried again, "I wasn't laughing at you. I know about the comic books. I have one, too."

"You do?"

"Only one. The first one."

Boyd stopped and turned to me. Because we were standing under a dark canopy of tree branches, I couldn't see his face clearly. But his voice was shaking. "You . . . *do?*"

"Yes," I said. "That's what brought me here. The cover of the book has a picture of the house. It's a long story and I don't even know what it is, really. We were here because my mom is selling the house—"

"That was you? With the sign?"

So he'd seen us that day. The boy next door had been watching. "Yes," I started.

"It's gone, you know. The next day the sign was gone."

"Oh," I said. My head was swimming with too many things and I was suddenly very, very cold. "Let's get out of here."

"Wait—I need to know. You said you have the first volume—"

"Yes," I said. "I brought it with me. It's in my

backpack—" and as the words left my mouth I suddenly remembered. "It's in the house."

"You left it in the house?! You had it and left it in the house?!"

"I had to," I said. "Something was biting me."

Boyd let out a long, loud breath and mumbled something about rats. "What?" I asked.

"It was his army of rats," he said.

This time I made sure I didn't laugh. "Come on," I said, "I want to get out of here." Something was starting to feel creepy in the woods.

Boyd took two steps, then stopped. The moon was back and I could see his face—he had the same look that my sister did when she came across a HARDEST JIGSAW piece that didn't quite make sense. "But you had it, so at least you know the story, right?"

"Well," I said. "I didn't really read the whole thing."

"You didn't read the whole thing?" He sounded like he was about to cry.

I grabbed his arm. "Come on, Boyd. I think we should move."

But Boyd remained perfectly still, like his feet had taken root right there in the middle of the forest. "If it's in the house, you can get it back."

"Are you crazy?" I remembered the smell of fresh paint. That tall, hulking figure. "There's somebody in there! Someone is hiding out in there!"

"I know. That's what I tried to tell you and you laughed at me. It's him. *He*'s living there." Boyd reached up and rubbed the top of his head nervously. "But, listen. He goes out at night. You could sneak back in and get it."

I was too tired, too cold, and too scared to even think about going back into that house. Plus, I had something else on my mind. Was it my imagination, or was there that same steady sound of footsteps I'd heard earlier? I closed my eyes and tried to listen past the normal nighttime rustlings of the forest.

"What?" said Boyd.

I opened my eyes. Boyd's hair was sticking straight up. "Well," I said quietly, "I think maybe I heard something."

"What?"

I put my finger to my lips and tried to fight the feeling I'd be lost in the forest forever, some sort of lesson for children for years to come. *Did you hear about the girl who went into the forest at night? Well, that was eighty-nine years ago and she's in there still.*

"Boyd," I whispered, "you have no idea how to get out of here, do you?"

"No," he whispered back.

Please, someone. Please, Tina Louise. Tell us what to do. I stood very still and waited for some kind of sign. Just when I thought she'd deserted me, Tina Louise swung backward from a tree branch and hung upside-down by the back of her knees. "If I were you," she whispered, "I'd run."

And that's when I heard it for certain—slow, steady, deliberate footsteps. For the third time in the longest day I ever hope to have, something was following me. So I took Tina Louise's advice. I grabbed Boyd's arm. "Run!" I said. And we did. We ran.

CHAPTER 27

YOU KNOW THAT DREAM where you run and run and run but don't get anywhere? I was living that dream for real. The shadows in the forest danced around us, as if they'd been set free by this wild chase in the night.

Arms pumping, chests heaving, Boyd and I ran side by side—so fast, our feet seemed to glide over the rough and uneven ground. But no matter how fast we ran I couldn't shake the feeling that something was right behind us, moving steadily, breathing easily, completely amused by our awkward flailings and sweaty efforts.

And then everything changed. It took me a moment to realize that the ground under my feet felt different. Smooth and hard and flat. And there were no trees in front of me.

"The road," Boyd said, like he didn't quite believe it, either.

"The road," I said, glancing down at the pavement, amazed by our luck. We'd stumbled out of the forest only a few hundred yards from Boyd's house!

Boyd started to laugh. "We made it!" he said. "We made it!"

Remembering my close call on the front porch, I yanked him by the sleeve. "We have to get inside,

Boyd." As I said it, there was another crash in the woods that sent us racing down the road.

I kept waiting for a hand to clamp down on my shoulder and yank me away, but it didn't come. And just moments after leaving the dark, wild forest, we were running across Boyd's lawn, up the front steps to a tidy porch with a happy-face welcome mat and automatic-security light. Which is where we stood, blinking at each other and wondering, *What next?*

From inside the house came the wake-up call for Boyd: the *stomp, stomp* of heavy feet. "Hide behind that bush," he said quickly. He gave me a gentle shove off the porch and added, "Then meet me at my bedroom window. Over there."

He barely had time to point to the side of the house before the front door opened and a man's voice called out, "Boyd? You still out there? It's just about bedtime, son."

I crouched behind the small bush next to the porch, but was only partially hidden. Boyd covered for me, blocking the doorway as much as he could. As the door shut I heard the voice once again. "See any more lights in the old house?" But I couldn't hear what Boyd said back.

It took me a moment to realize what had just happened and that I was outside, alone, with nothing but the porch light for safety and comfort. The idea of leaving that small circle of light was unbearable—like leaving a campfire in freezing weather. But I knew I had no choice.

I crept along the side of the house, moving toward what I hoped was Boyd's bedroom window. Then, I crouched down, hugged my arms to my chest, and waited.

How funny. That very morning I'd woken up in my own bed in my own room. I'd had cornflakes for breakfast, just like any other morning. Then, instead of walking my little sister to school, I'd waved good-bye to her at the corner and caught the bus to the ferry. And now I was waiting outside a strange boy's window. How funny that everything could change so quickly.

I heard a window open above my head and then a whisper. "Hey!" I looked up to see Boyd grinning down at me. He held out his hand and I took it. He yanked and I climbed and somehow we managed to get me up the five feet or so to his bedroom window. For the second time in one day, Mrs. P.E. would have been proud.

I tumbled over the window ledge into a place so safe and warm I wanted to cry. "Thank you—" I started, but before I could finish, Boyd put his finger to his mouth and pushed me across the room. He opened the door to his closet and flicked on the light. "Hide in here until I come back," he whispered, reaching under his shirt and bringing out three slices of dark brown bread. "It's the best thing we have around here," he added.

"Thanks," I said, biting into a slice. It was chewy and dry, but I ate it gratefully. "Where are you going?"

"I have to empty the garbage. I'll be quick." He closed the door softly, leaving me alone with my three slices of dry, brown bread and the largest collection of comic books I'd ever seen.

CHAPTER 28

BEFORE MY MOM GOT so tired, we spent a lot of time cleaning out closets. "You can tell everything about a person by the state of their closet," Lizzie would say, standing in front of ours and pointing out things we might have missed. She believed in organizer bags for shoes, organizer boxes for sweaters, and organizer shelves for everything else.

I wondered what someone would think of me if they had to spend an hour in my closet now. Piles of rumpled clothes, stacks of overdue library books, and, of course, my poster board project of killer lap dogs.

Boyd's closet, on the other hand, was any mother's dream. Shirts on hangers, shoes in a row with their toes pointing in the same direction, even his vast collection of comics was organized so that the spines all lined up perfectly. What did these books have to do with me? Why was one sent to my mother four years ago?

I pulled a volume from the pile and opened to the middle. For the first time I noticed how beautiful the binding was and how thick and soft the paper felt between my fingers. The colors, too, were unlike any I'd seen in a book before. Reds as deep and real as ripe berries and blues that seemed to change right there on the page like a windy spring sky. Even black was a color to notice—so dark and alive it seemed to be scooped straight out of a moonless night. The boxed drawings were like carefully tended garden plots, each growing something slightly different than the one next to it. I brought the book close to my face, closed my eyes and sniffed. Paint. It smelled of paint.

Boyd threw open the closet door and stared at me, then at the books I'd spread out on the floor. The expression on his face made shivers run up my back.

Why was he so upset? Was it the books? "Boyd, I'm sorry—" I started, then stopped.

Boyd was shaking his head back and forth. He opened his mouth several times, but no words came out.

"What?" I asked, watching his pale face. "What's the matter?"

With trembling hands, Boyd held out a sheet of paper. Even before I looked down at it, I knew. The moment my fingers felt it, they knew. It was that strange paper—thick and soft—the same paper as in the book I'd just been holding. "Where did you get this?" I asked, not quite believing what I was seeing.

"It was on the porch just now," Boyd managed to squeak. "When I went to empty the garbage."

I looked at it again, trying to put all my jumbled thoughts in some kind of order. "That's us, Boyd," I said finally, out loud, even though it was the most obvious thing I could say. "That's us in the woods just now. That's us."

"I know," he whispered. "I know."

I looked at the sheet of paper again—the two kids in the comics were us, no doubt about it, even down to the shoelaces.

"Now do you believe?" Boyd couldn't take his eyes away.

"I believe what I believed before—that someone wants to scare me away from the house."

"Of course he does," Boyd said. "Of course. How else could he have survived all these years?"

Remembering what had happened earlier when I laughed about the Ratt, I kept my mouth shut. But Boyd pressed on. "I can't believe it. He drew me. There we are—being attacked by his army of rats!" He stared at the sheet of paper, eyes glowing.

I was confused. "You seem happy about it," I said. "Are you happy about it?"

Boyd didn't answer. He turned his face away from me and carefully tucked the slip of paper into one of the comics in the pile. Then he reached to the top shelf of his closet and pulled down a pillow and blanket. "My Dad will be in here any minute. You should probably get under the bed so we can talk." He stepped out of the closet and ran to his bed. "Okay," he said, pulling the covers up over his jeans and sweatshirt. "Hurry."

I glanced nervously at the open door leading out to the hallway. "Wouldn't it be safer if you closed the bedroom door?" I whispered.

"It's never closed," he said simply. But there was something in the way he said it. Maybe he was like Sophie. Maybe he was afraid of the dark.

I grabbed the blanket and pillow and dashed across the carpeted floor. Then I dropped to my knees and rolled underneath his bed. The carpet was soft and thick and warm. I fluffed the pillow under my head and pulled the blanket up to my neck.

"Okay, Margaret," Boyd whispered down to me, wasting no time. "What were you doing in the mansion?"

I thought for a moment, staring at the sagging underside of Boyd's bed, just a few inches from my face. I'd never been underneath a bed before, and it made me feel like I was the only person in the world. "It's a long story," I said finally.

"Okay," he said. "I'm listening."

I tried to think of a lie, but when I opened my mouth, what came out was the truth. Maybe it was because I couldn't see his face—or maybe it was because I'd seen it so clearly earlier on the front porch—

but I heard myself telling this strange boy all about my life back home. I told him about my little sister and my sleepy, chain-smoking mother. I told him about school and my poster-board report, and about Tina Louise peeing her pants. I told him about Fate and the package I found on the back porch of the mansion. And then, finally, I told him about my dad. The mystery of my dad.

"He drowned? Drowned out here?" Boyd sounded like he'd had the wind knocked out of him.

"Yes," I said, startled. I'd almost forgotten he was up there listening.

"Drowned," he said again. The bedsprings creaked above me.

"Shut up," I said.

"What? Why?"

"Just shut up." I had the feeling that he was looking straight into my heart and the sad little question hiding there. *Did you really want to come back to us, Dad?*

"No, listen," Boyd said quickly. "I'm sorry about your dad. I didn't mean it like that. But it's just—do you know about the Drowning Ghost? Do you remember reading about the Drowning Ghost?"

"I mean it," I said. "I don't want to talk anymore."

"No," said Boyd, "you don't get what I'm trying to say. Maybe if you'd read it carefully, you'd already know that it was the Drowning Ghost that probably got him. Maybe if you knew the story you wouldn't be telling me to shut up."

I took a deep breath, just like Tina Louise would have told me to do. This boy knew something about the house next door. He had the comic books and he'd been watching the place. "Okay, then," I said, trying to keep my voice steady. "Maybe it's your turn. Maybe you should tell me the story."

CHAPTER 29

BOYD SCRAMBLED OUT OF bed and ran to his closet. "What are you doing?" Margaret called, but he didn't answer. A moment later and with an arm full of comics, Boyd bounced back into bed, spread the books across his comforter and cleared his throat nervously. He'd never had the chance to talk about Ratt like this with anyone before and he didn't quite know where to start. The kids at school all laughed at him for reading them ("Did you draw that yourself, rat boy?") and his parents weren't interested. Mr. Librarian was always too busy with his scrapbooks to talk much. And then, this girl shows up—this girl with the key to the mansion and a copy of *Ratt Volume 1*. What could be more amazing, more unbelievable, more exciting?

"Okay," Boyd began timidly. "Well, once there were two boys, about our age. They were best of friends— you could call them brothers, actually, and they did everything together."

How could he do this right? He closed his eyes and the two boys stood in front of him. In a moment, he knew, they would come to life for him. They always did.

"See," he continued slowly, "the Drowning Ghost was a regular person when he was a kid, just like you and me. Except he was an excellent swimmer. I mean, he was like a fish. A human fish. And he and the Ratt were friends. This was before the Ratt was a rat. He was just a boy, too. They lived in this mortal world, but had their own world going on at the same time. Because they were different than everyone else. Each one was special."

Margaret called up from beneath the bed, "What do you mean by special?"

Boyd opened his eyes. "Well, like I said, one could swim. It sort of made him a hero with all the other kids."

"And the other one?"

"The other one, he sort of looked like a rat. All the kids at school teased him and called him 'rat boy,' because he had little eyes that were close together and his chin and mouth sort of made a point. He only had one friend—the boy who could swim. So one day after the rat boy had been teased to the point of tears, his friend tried to cheer him up by saying, 'Hey, let's both be rats. Really rats.' See, the swimming boy was compassionate to a fault. He would rather turn himself into something disgusting than see the rat boy suffer alone. So they formed a secret Rat Club. And they did secret assignments, like scavenge for things. They'd walk home from school together and look for stuff on the road—stuff that other people had just thrown away or lost without even knowing it. And they'd take it home and clean it up and make the most amazing things. That's what they called their mission."

Boyd shuffled through his pile of comics and pulled out *Ratt Volume 2*. He opened to a picture of two boys and handed it down to Margaret, along with the flashlight he kept next to his bed. He watched her until he thought his head would burst from being upside-down. Then he sat back up and waited for her reaction.

"He doesn't look *that* much like a rat," she said finally.

Boyd sighed. "Just wait," he said. "Just wait."

"But, Boyd. A person can't really turn into a rat."

"Do you want to hear the rest of the story, or do you want to argue with me?"

"I want to hear the story," Margaret mumbled.

"Okay, then." And as Boyd continued with the story, his voice grew stronger, more confident and sure. Reds and blues and blacks began to swirl together, making the pictures come to life. Two boys walked down a dusty road together, arm-in-arm.

"One day the boys stumbled onto something that would change their world. It was a junkyard. Now instead of waiting to come across something that had been tossed in a can or dumped along the side of the road, they went straight to the junkyard and found more stuff than they would ever know what to do with. It was like an entire football field full of treasures— lost, overlooked, abandoned.

"They decided to spend every day after school in the junkyard. They couldn't believe what people would throw away. All the things in the world, all the wonderful things—piling up, just to make room for new. The two boys would take them home and clean them up and make them beautiful again. Truly beautiful. And useful. And better than before. It was all they thought about, day and night. They couldn't concentrate at school, thinking about the junkyard and what might be laying underneath a sheet of plastic or a pile of concrete."

"Like what?"

"Like stuff. All stuff."

"Like balls of twine and mannequin hands?"

"Yeah," said Boyd. "Anyway, this went on until their parents discovered how they were spending their time after school. They found the stash, gathered all the wonderful things the boys had fixed up, put it all in boxes and dumped it back at the junkyard. All the shiny pieces of metal and the freshly scrubbed wheels. Even the super-deluxe bicycle they'd put together from broken pieces of at least fifty different bicycles. All it needed was a seat—just a seat and it would have been perfect, even better than new. But their parents loaded up even their nearly perfect bicycle and took it all back to the junkyard. Then, when the boys cried, their parents bought them each a brand-new, shiny bike—one blue, one red. And the boys cried even more. Do you see the picture, Margaret?" Boyd called down. "Are you on the right page?"

"Yes," she said, "I see it."

Boyd continued. "Now. Even though they were very good boys and truly wanted to obey their parents, the thought of the junkyard loomed big in their minds. They couldn't eat, they couldn't sleep, they couldn't concentrate in school. All they could think about were the things that were being thrown away, every minute of every day. Things that still had life in them. Finally they made a plan: They would sneak out at night, when their parents thought they were tucked away in bed. They would sneak out at night and go back to the junkyard."

Boyd took a deep breath and closed his eyes. He knew the story by heart and loved saying every single word. And this part was one of his favorites. "Have you ever seen a junkyard at night? Underneath a full moon? Well, it glows. It glows with things aching to be touched, to be rescued and restored. And the boys did. They touched, they rescued, they made better than new. And doing this made the boys happy for many, many months. But then something started to change. It changed so slowly that, at first, neither one noticed." Boyd stopped. He rifled through the books, searching for the right one, then realized it was still under the bed with Margaret.

"Why did you stop?"

"Hand me the book."

Margaret tossed the book up onto the bed.

"Hey, careful!" Boyd picked it up gently and opened to a page near the end. "Look at it closely," he said, handing it back down.

"Okay," said Margaret. She took the book and shone the flashlight on the pictures. The two boys were still in the junkyard, but something had changed. One boy was happily digging through bags of garbage and rotting food. The other boy reached for what looked like a lovely round ball, but the minute he picked it up, it dissolved into a mess of rotting goo. He looked like he was going to vomit.

"For the rat boy," Boyd said, "nothing had changed. About the junkyard, anyway. He loved it as much as he ever had, probably more. But the other boy. He started looking at garbage as, well, garbage— as something that should be thrown away and never touched again. Something that was disgusting and smelly. And every night it got harder and harder for him to sneak into the junkyard and bring the things home. He just didn't want to touch it anymore. He couldn't help it, really. It wasn't his fault—it was just something that happened. See, for the first time ever, garbage smelled bad to him."

"Oh," said Margaret. A sadness had crept into her voice.

Boyd continued. "Now, that part was easy to understand. After all, most people don't want to touch garbage. But what happened next, what happened to the other boy—well, neither one could have antici- pated or explained. See, he, too, was changing, but in a very different way."

"Hair was starting to sprout up from the back of his hands. A fine line of fuzz appeared along the tops of his ears, and his nose and mouth began to point out from his face. He couldn't eat food unless it was beginning to rot.

"His parents ignored it for as long as they could, but finally, even they had to admit something was wrong."

"He had to wear three pairs of socks, or his new sharp toenails would scratch the hardwood floors."

"There wasn't a dentist on the island who would even look at his teeth. They were afraid of getting rabies."

"And while some might say, 'Human beings can't really turn into rats,' or, 'It's called puberty, stupid!'

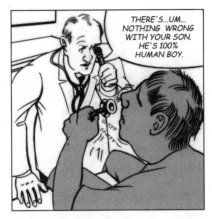

or better yet—"

"—the truth was, it was true. The boy was turning into a rat. And while the rat boy was going through this huge transformation, the other boy, well, he was going through a change of his own. People started to notice that he was an amazing swimmer. He broke record after school record. He could swim two entire lengths of the pool without taking a breath. He could swim for three hours straight. He was becoming, quite simply, a hero."

The drawing took my breath away. I held the book closer to get a better look. It was of a boy, surrounded by friends and fans. Just out of the pool, he was glistening with water, grinning, and holding up a medal—the same medal that, at that very moment, was hanging around my little sister's neck.

I hugged the book to my chest. Tears welled up from somewhere inside, like they'd been on call and waiting. I tried to blink them away, but one managed to get loose. I felt it slide slowly down the side of my nose. *Could that be you, Dad?* I whispered to the boy in the comic. I'd only seen photographs of him as a grown-up man, so I couldn't be sure. But the medal was the same. Exactly the same.

"Hey." I heard the bedsprings creak and suddenly Boyd's face was upside-down and looking at me. "What's wrong?"

"Nothing," I said.

"Give me the flashlight. Are you crying?"

"No." I turned it off so he couldn't see my face.

"You are, too. You're crying." Just then Boyd's dad came booming down the hall. *Stomp, stomp, stomp.* "Shhh," Boyd whispered.

From underneath the bed I watched as big brown slippers stepped into the room. "Is everything all right, son?"

"Yeah, Dad. Sure."

"You still seeing lights in that house?"

"No, they went away. I mean, you were right. They were never there in the first place."

Stomp, stomp, stomp. Squeak, creak. Boyd's dad sat down on the edge of the bed. "What's the old rat man up to tonight?"

"Same old stuff, Dad. Finding junk, fixing junk."

"And you got all your homework done?"

"Got it done before dinner."

"Okay, well, sleep well, son. No nightmares."

"You too, Dad. Good night."

Creak, squeak. I heard Boyd's dad lean over and kiss him good night. I watched his feet walk back across the floor. I swear I could almost hear Boyd holding his breath.

"Boyd?" I asked as soon as the feet had disappeared into the hallway.

"Not so loud."

"What about the Drowning Ghost?"

"All I know," Boyd said, "is that he is Ratt's best friend, all grown up. All I know is that somehow the two best friends are now deadly enemies. And every month, when the moon is full, the Drowning Ghost comes out. He comes out to search for eyes because the crabs and bottom fish have eaten his out of his head. So he sneaks up behind anyone out on the water. Their only warning is a long, slow chill down the back of their neck—the icy finger of the Drowning Ghost. But once they've felt it, it's too late—he has them in his death clutch and is pulling them down, down, down. Down to the bottom of the sea, where he will scoop out their eyes and make them his own. And, until the small crabs and bottom fish sniff out these new eyes, the Drowning Ghost can see. For a few days he can see. And he uses that sight to try and obtain the one thing he wants most in this world."

Boyd paused dramatically, waiting for some sort of reaction from me. "Okay," I finally managed to whisper, "what is it he wants?"

"Revenge," Boyd answered. "Revenge for the life he has lost."

A long, slow chill ran down the back of my neck. "And how exactly? How did he lose his life?"

"That," Boyd answered smugly, "is what you could have told me."

"What do you mean?"

"You had the answer—it's in *Ratt Volume 1*. You had it in your hand. You left it in the house."

CHAPTER 30

BOYD HAD WANTED TO talk more after that, but I told him I was too sleepy and that we could talk in the morning. The truth was I just wanted time to sort things out for myself.

I had wanted to tell him. The words "I think my dad was that swim champ" were right there, so close to coming out. But something made me keep silent. The silence made my chest hurt, but I kept my mouth shut anyway.

There was just something so strange about Boyd—the way he'd told me the story. It was like he was telling me something real, something he believed was as true as his own first day of school or how his mom met his dad. So if I was right, if the young swim champ really was my father, then that would mean he was also the Drowning Ghost—at least, in Boyd's make-believe world. And that's the last place I wanted him to be.

Even with so much to think about, I must have fallen asleep, because the next thing I knew it was morning. Someone was placing a piece of toast by my ear and whispering, "We're all leaving now. Don't mess anything up."

I rolled over to my side and looked blankly at the

toast. Why was I under the bed? Where was Sophie? Why hadn't she woken me with her head alarm? Whose feet were those?

Then in an instant my mind snapped awake and everything from the day before came back to me. The shadowy figure in the mansion, running into Boyd on the street and again in the woods, the menacing drawing left on the front porch.

I heard Boyd's mother shout out from the living room that the bus was coming. "Hey—" I started.

"I gotta go," he said, feet moving away from the bed.

"Wait! What am I going to do? We have to come up with a plan."

"I don't have time."

"Boyd, wait. I—"

"I'll see you later, Margaret," he whispered quickly. And then he was gone, leaving the bedroom door wide open behind him.

I curled up in a tight little ball and nibbled on a corner of the toast, waiting out the last of the morning sounds—toilets flushing, doors slamming, cars starting. Then, when I was sure I was completely alone in the house, I rolled out from underneath the bed.

Was I really here? Had I really been chased through the woods and spent the night in a stranger's house? Would I really not be walking my little sister to school that morning and suiting up for P.E.? I stretched my arms up over my head and glanced at the window—and that's when any feeling of freedom and excitement left me. The moment I saw the mansion, it was like I'd been dunked in ice water.

With a shiver I moved away from the window and crossed the room to the bedroom door. A small hallway connected the bedroom to the rest of the house, with two doorways on either side of the hallway. The first door opened to Boyd's parents' room; the second to a tidy, blue-and-yellow bathroom.

I stepped into the bathroom and turned on the light. There was a girl in the mirror, but she didn't look like me. Her wild, tangled hair was full of pine needles and twigs; she had dirt on her nose and a scratch on her chin; the neck of her white T-shirt was filthy. I looked into her surprised eyes and almost laughed out loud. Was this really me? It wasn't me yesterday.

Because the yellow washcloths were too nice, I used my hands to splash water on my face. Then I brushed my teeth using my index finger and some funny-tasting, all-natural toothpaste. I worked a comb through my matted hair and found a rubber band to tie it back in a ponytail. Then I looked in the mirror again. Besides the grubby T-shirt and dusty jeans, I looked pretty much like myself again.

I turned off the light, stepped out of the bathroom and wandered down the rest of the hallway. Family pictures almost completely covered the walls, and I stopped to study each one of them: Boyd sitting on

Santa's lap, Boyd and his dad building a sand castle on the beach, Boyd and his mom smiling in front of the Grand Canyon. If Lizzie ever got around to taking photos, what would go on our family wall? Sophie riding in a shopping cart? Me sorting out whites? I suddenly missed Sophie, more than I ever thought I could. Her skinny arms and missing teeth. Her dark brown eyes.

In the living room I spotted a telephone, which was good since all my quarters for calling home were in the backpack in the mansion. I looked at my watch and dialed the number. My heart was beating fast. What if Sophie wasn't there? What if something had happened to her on the way home from school yesterday? She picked up on the first ring. "Sophie?" I said.

"Margaret!" she cried. "I knew it was you!"

I heard a muffled noise in the background. "Is that Mom?"

Sophie giggled. "She just yelled for us to stop our fighting. I'm doing a good job, aren't I?"

"You're doing a perfect job, Sophie." I pictured her in the kitchen, eating a big bowl of pink cereal.

"Where are you, anyway?" she asked.

"I'm at a house. The house next door."

"When are you coming home?"

"Soon. Does Mom suspect anything?"

"No. I stomp around the kitchen when she's in the living room. She thinks it's you. Did you find out the mystery?"

"Not yet, but I'm getting close. The house just had a lot of junk. You're not missing a thing." I pressed the phone to my ear and closed my eyes. I could hear Sophie's loud breath on the other end. There was nothing to say, really, but I wasn't ready to hang up. "How's school?" I asked.

"Fine. Should I give a message to Tina Louise for you?"

"No," I said, then changed my mind. I knew how happy it would make Sophie to give her one. "Yes. Just tell her—tell her she was right. About Fate."

"Okay," said Sophie, trying to keep the conversation going. "It seems like you've been gone a long time."

"I know. But it's only been a day, Sophie."

"Will you call me again?"

"I don't know," I said. "I lost my quarters."

"Oh." Disappointed.

"Okay, Sophie? Are you okay?" She didn't answer. "Sophie are you nodding your head?" Still no answer. "You know I can't hear you when you nod your head. Are you okay?"

"Yes," she said finally. "I'm okay."

"Okay, Sophie. 'Bye."

"'Bye, Margaret."

I hung up the phone and felt both better and worse. I could almost see my little sister standing there still, the phone pressed against her ear, waiting for something more.

I wandered back to Boyd's bedroom and sat down on the bed, trying to think of what to do next. Going back to the mansion was out of the question, and I wasn't ready to turn around and take the ferry home—especially since I now had more questions than when I arrived.

Even though the original plan had been to do this alone, I couldn't get Boyd out of my head—Boyd and the strange story he'd told me.

I knew there was something I wasn't seeing clearly, but the more I tried to focus, the fuzzier it all got. There was the comic book world and the real world. In the comic book world was a boy with the same swim medal as my father; in the real world someone was trying to scare me away from the house. What I needed was to stay in the real world and find the facts—and there had to be facts.

The librarian. Whoever wrote the comics brought them into the library, so the librarian must know something. I thought about the funny little man, his long pair of scissors and the way he lied about having old newspapers. I jumped up. At least it was a place to start.

I needed to find Boyd—but how to get back to town? I had no idea how the island bus system worked, and I certainly wasn't about to try and walk the whole way again. Hitchhiking was too scary. What would Tina Louise do? I sat back down on the bed and took a deep breath, just like she taught me. I closed my eyes and waited. And that's when I thought to go have a look in the garage.

I was four when I first tried to ride a bike. My mother was going to find little training wheels to help me get started, but my dad couldn't wait. One day he took me and the bike out on the sidewalk in front of our house. I remember I was wearing a red-and-white checkered dress, which now strikes me as a very funny thing to be wearing on the first day of learning to ride a bike. My dad set me on the bike and placed my feet on the pedals (they *almost* reached). He grabbed the handlebars and told me to hang on tight. Then he started to run. Up and down the street we went, my dad pushing until he was out of breath and too tired to run anymore. I didn't learn to ride that day, and I don't remember exactly when I did. What I will always remember is that first time of trying, my dad gripping the handlebars and running alongside the bike while my legs hung uselessly over the sides; the red-and-white checked pattern of my dress as it billowed around me, and the feeling that something magical was about to happen, I just didn't know what. It's the story Sophie likes to hear when she's sad.

Boyd's bike was a twelve-speed, with big fat tires for riding on dirt trails, though there wasn't a speck of dirt on them anywhere. I pulled the bike from the corner of the garage and walked it across the front lawn, the big fat tires making a winding-snake pattern on the wet grass. My heart did a flip-flop as I rode past the mansion, but as soon as I was out of sight down the road, it settled right down.

Editor's Note:

It's important that I interrupt for just a moment here. Let's say that, instead of Margaret, this story is really about Sophie. Because, you see, Sophie isn't aware that it's not. She doesn't know that it's not the story of a little girl whose big sister runs away to an island, leaving her all alone. She doesn't know that she's not the hero. She doesn't know that this next part could be cut out because it's not from the point-of-view of our main character, now is it? In Sophie's world, she is the main character and the main character is tired of waiting for her runaway sister to come home. So in Sophie's story, what happens after the phone call from her sister might go something like this:

"Mom, Margaret ran away. She went to see what was in the house."

"Stop it, Sophie. I'm tired of your jokes."

"It's not a joke."

"Aren't you going to be late for school? Where's Margaret?"

"I told you. She went to the house. Is that where our dad died?"

"I'm already late for work."

"Mom, tell me. Is that where he died?"

"Yes, Sophie, okay? That's where he died."

"Who killed him?"

"Sophie! Nobody killed him. Who said anything about killing? Go eat something. Did you have breakfast? What's in the fridge?"

"Peanut butter."

"Go make yourself a sandwich."

"But it's a dangerous place?"

"Yes, it's a very dangerous place. That's why I didn't let you go in. Go tell Margaret to make you a peanut butter sandwich. You can eat it on the way."

"I can't, Mom. She's—there's no milk."

And after a scene like that, Sophie might run all the way to Holy Names Academy, beating the first bell. She might scan the crowd, looking for Tina Louise. Maybe she'd find her off in a corner of the playfield, maybe alone, maybe with some big blond boy holding a baseball and a bat. Sophie would, of course, tell Tina Louise about the telephone call from her sister and about the conversation with her mother. She'd stress the fact that the house on the island was, indeed, a very dangerous place.

Tina Louise might nod and say something about Fate. How when Fate speaks, for example, one should listen.

So Sophie might stand perfectly still and wait for Fate to speak once again. "I think," she might say after a moment of waiting, "that Fate has just told me to go find my sister." After that, she might run home and pack a suitcase with the things she would need for an adventure of such magnitude: a pair of socks, an extra sweatshirt, a box of frozen burritos, and THE HARDEST JIGSAW EVER MADE. Then she would wait—either patiently or impatiently—for the bus that would take her to the ferry.

CHAPTER 31

BOYD'S PHYSICAL EDUCATION teacher knew how to organize only three sports—softball, soccer, and track and field—and each week he rotated between the three. Boyd could tell which week it was by the color of the bruises on his shins—by the time they were light brown and barely visible, it was time for soccer again.

Fortunately, this week was track and field and, of the three, it was the one Boyd hated the least. He always signed up for distance running (he was the only one) and spent the entire class racing in huge circles around the playfield.

Distance running freed his mind and, after about the third lap around, Boyd would find himself floating above the grass and dirt of the playfield and the shouts and squirmishes of his classmates. It was as close as he could get to flying, and he loved the feeling. Up high like that, his classmates didn't look so frightening. They couldn't call him names or tease him about his comics or chase him with sticks. When he was up high he felt strong and brave. Like a super-hero.

On this particular day, though, Boyd was finding it difficult to drift away. As he circled the perimeter of the schoolyard, he tried to fight the feeling that something was anchoring him to the ground. He scanned the field. As usual, his classmates looked like colorful patches against the muted greens and browns. The only group that really stood out was the Threes—and that was because, as usual, they had signed up for javelin and were waving it around like a weapon.

As he circled again he noticed a small figure standing next to a bicycle outside the chain-link fence. Hmmm. Too small to be a grown-up, but why would a kid be standing outside the playfield during school hours? Even though it was the last thing he wanted to do, he let the wind carry him down for a closer look.

Closer, closer, until he could make out that the figure standing outside the fence was Margaret. But what would Margaret be doing at his school? Had something happened? Boyd felt a funny lurch in his stomach as he let himself be pulled all the way to the ground.

CHAPTER 32

I LEANED THE BIKE against the chain-link fence and watched them. Except for the fact that no one was wearing a uniform, this could have been my P.E. class back home. I spotted Boyd right away, running around the playground like some wild thing was chasing him, but as far as I could see, no one was paying him the slightest bit of attention.

"Boyd!" I called, but he was too far away to hear me. I watched him turn the corner and sprint past three boys holding what looked like a spear. I shuddered. If I was home right now, I'd be standing with a baseball bat on my shoulder.

"Hey, you!"

I looked up. It was the spear boys, grinning wickedly and pointing their sharp thing in my direction. I looked around. Since there was no one behind me and no one next to me, I was pretty sure they were pointing it at me. "Hey, you!" they shouted again. Now they were moving across the playground with big, purposeful strides. The spear glinted in the sunlight.

"This is a little weird," I heard Tina Louise whisper as the spear boys moved close enough to show the numbers spelled out on their shirts—One, Two, Three.

I heard another voice, but this time it wasn't in my head. And it was telling me to run.

"Run, Margaret!" Waving his arms frantically, Boyd raced across the playground shouting, "Run, Margaret, run!"

I jumped on his bike, turned and pedaled. This time I didn't need to imagine a pack of miniature dogs or a swarm of killer bees right behind me and closing in. I pedaled like I was being chased by three strong boys carrying one long spear.

CHAPTER 33

"WHY'D YOU TELL HER to run?" After Margaret's escape, the Threes had cornered Boyd. The P.E. teacher had saved him out on the playfield, then turned around and done the unthinkable: sent all four into the locker room together for some "cooling off time." Now, red-faced and angry, the Threes had Boyd pinned against a cold, metal locker. "Why'd you tell her to run?" they demanded again.

Boyd tried to look away. His hair was still wet from the shower and he was shivering. "I don't know," he mumbled.

"Is she your girlfriend?" One laughed, and when One laughed, Two and Three always joined him.

Three shoved Boyd in the chest. "Speak, rat boy."

Boyd glanced up at the clock. The P.E. teacher and the other kids would be coming in any minute. He tried to move his face away from the hot breath of the Threes, but they only pressed in closer. *What would the Ratt do in a situation like this?* he asked himself. *What would Boyd the superhero do?* He probably would not say a word. He probably would just lift off the ground with his fabulous flying powers, circle high above them and—spit.

Before he knew what he was doing, before he had time to think and tell himself *STOP, YOU IDIOT,*

STOP!, a big fat wad of spit left Boyd's mouth, traveling at a nearly supersonic speed. Like a shiny round bullet it seemed to split the air in two as it headed for its target: the wide-open laughing mouth of One.

"Ahhhhhh!" One fell to his knees, grabbed at his throat and choked in agony.

The few boys who had just trickled in from the playfield couldn't help themselves—they burst out laughing. Even Two and Three laughed, before they realized what they were doing.

One was still on the ground, gagging and choking on Boyd's spit, but Boyd knew he'd be back on his feet in moments. Acting on pure impulse, Boyd leapfrogged over One's back and made a dash for the locker-room door.

At that very moment, the P.E. teacher stepped into the locker room. "No running in the locker room!" he shouted, but by then Boyd had already flown past him and was halfway out the door.

He ran and didn't slow down, not even when he was far from the chain-link fence that encircled the school grounds.

CHAPTER 34

THERE I WAS, STANDING in the middle of a strange road, next to a pasture of strange cows, holding up a twelve-speed bike and listening to two words play over and over in my head. *Stand still.*

It was what Lizzie used to tell Sophie. "If you're ever lost in an amusement park, don't come looking for me. Stand still and I will find you." I always thought that was a funny thing for her to say since I don't remember even once going to an amusement park. But Sophie would nod her head solemnly and promise that she would do just that.

Stand still. I closed my eyes, waiting for more words that would help me know what to do. Words didn't come, but images did. I saw my father in his white T-shirt and faded jeans, grinning and holding out his hand. I saw the mansion, a key, a blue canoe bobbing on white-capped water. I saw my mother's face looking worried, even with her eyes closed. I saw D.J., a glistening spear, Sophie with a swimming medal around her neck.

When I opened my eyes, there he was. "How'd you know where to find me?" I asked. For some reason, I wasn't even surprised.

Boyd grinned. His hair was wet and sticking up all

over his head. "I don't know," he said. "Somehow I just ended up here."

Fate.

We stood in the middle of the gravel road with cows so close I could have touched their damp noses. Suddenly, I wanted to laugh.

"Why are you smiling?"

"I don't know." I looked around. The tall grass in the pasture was honey-colored brown. "I've never been so close to cows before." And then I added, "Or boys chasing me with a spear." How could I say it? *Because you found me again, that's why.*

"A javelin," he corrected.

"Whatever. It was sharp."

"I know."

"Who were they, anyway?"

"They call themselves the Threes. One, Two, and Three."

I nodded. He didn't have to say anything more. We turned and started back down the road. I asked him what had happened after I'd run.

He shook his head. "Nothing." But he said it the way Lizzie does when she doesn't want to talk anymore. I looked down at my feet making a funny pattern with the fat bike tire.

"Do you have a canoe?" I asked, thinking of the very first day and the rickety little dock.

"No," said Boyd.

"You know that one tied to the dock? The shiny blue one?" When he didn't answer, I asked again.

"I don't go down to the water much," he said.

"Why not?"

"I don't know." Then he said, "Because of the Drowning Ghost."

"Oh." I thought about the story he'd told me the night before. The only thing that seemed real was the fat tire crunching along the road and the humming of bumblebees.

"I know it sounds stupid."

"No it doesn't," I lied.

"My dad just bought a new motorboat, even," he said.

I didn't know what to say. "Well, I was just thinking about the canoe. I was thinking that whoever scared me from the house must go out in it. Maybe he fishes. We could watch from your window—"

"No," Boyd answered. "Ratt scavenges for food. In the dead of night."

"Right," I said. "Okay, something else, then. Mr. Librarian. He must know who brings in the books—"

"No, he doesn't."

"How do you know?"

Boyd looked uncomfortable. "I've asked him."

"Okay, then this. Have you ever noticed his scrapbooks? You know—the ones titled RAINFALL, SPORTS, MARRIAGES? Stuff like that?"

Boyd shook his head, but he wouldn't look at me.

"I want to read them."

"Impossible," said Boyd, kicking up tiny bits of gravel. "He never leaves the door unlocked."

"But does he ever leave?"

"Yes. Every day at three."

"And how do you know?"

"Because I'm there after school. I go with him to the drugstore for his box of donuts. Then I come back and read until I catch the sports bus home."

"And he locks the door when he leaves?"

"Yes."

"I need to get in there. I need to read them."

"Why?"

"Because—don't you see? If something happened to my dad out here—and I'm sure it did—then there must be an article about it."

"I don't know—"

"Boyd! There's a scrapbook labeled DEATH. There's one with the word MURDER."

"You think your dad was murdered?"

"I don't know what I think." I was all worked up now, and seeing spots of light when I blinked my eyes. "I know my dad is somehow connected to the mansion. I know my dad drowned. I know that someone chased me out of the house last night and left a threatening comic on your doorstep."

Boyd still wouldn't look at me.

I changed my tactic. Keeping my voice calm I said, "Don't you want to find out more about the Drowning

Ghost? Something that's not in the Ratt books?" Boyd lifted his head a tiny bit.

So I kept going. I told him my idea. How if Boyd could somehow manage to divert Mr. Librarian, I could look for any information about my father. "And," I added, "the Drowning Ghost, of course."

Boyd looked up at the sky and squinted. "You'd need a lot of time to look through everything," he said, almost to himself. "More than just five minutes."

"You're right," I said gently, trying not to push. *Come on, Boyd. Come on.*

"Well," he said finally, "maybe I know what you could do." And then he told me of an idea he'd once had about hiding in the library until Mr. Librarian closed up for the night. "I was never really going to do it, though," he added. "I just liked the idea."

"But it would work."

"I think it would. If he would just let me stay in the library while he went out for donuts, I could hide you in there. You could stay as long as you need."

"Right," I said. "Perfect." And as I said it, the cows mooed, the sun shone, and the gravel made a lovely crunching sound under our feet. At that moment the idea really did seem like a perfect one.

CHAPTER 35

"NEVER ENDING, NEVER ENDING," Mr. Librarian mumbled, slamming his scrapbook shut.

"What?" asked Boyd from his perch in the Rs. He glanced up at the clock on the wall. It was time.

"Nothing," said the librarian. He opened his desk drawer and took out a big chain of keys.

"Can I stay here today?"

"You don't want to go to the drugstore? You don't want to get the donuts with me?"

"I don't feel like it today."

Mr. Librarian narrowed his eyes. He looked Boyd up and down. "Are you sick?"

"No. I just want to read this story again before the bus comes."

Mr. Librarian nodded his head.

"Unless I could check out an extra one today—"

But Mr. Librarian didn't let him finish. "One is the limit. You know that. I never understand libraries that let a person check out three, four, even five at a time. What kind of a person can *read* five books at a time?"

Boyd shook his head. He'd heard it all before. He'd even once argued for changing the rules just on Friday, so he wouldn't run out of books over the weekend, but Mr. Librarian had instead decided to change his hours of business. He was now open seven days a week.

"So can I stay here and finish? Just this once?"

Mr. Librarian scratched the side of his nose. "What will you do if another patron comes in?"

Even though that had never happened before, Boyd answered respectfully, "I'll tell them to take a look around and that you'll be back in five minutes. You're alphabetical by topic, except for poetry."

"And if there's any funny business?"

"Then I'll call you," Boyd said. "At the drugstore."

Mr. Librarian nodded his head slowly. "Okay," he said finally. "Okay."

"Okay," Boyd said back, trying not to sound as relieved as he felt. Or as nervous.

Mr. Librarian took one last look around, then walked to the door. "Three o'clock comes earlier every day," he mumbled as he headed out the door and down the street. Boyd waited for the last jingle of the bell, then sprang into action. He ran to the front of the library, peeked through the curtain and waved his arms wildly.

CHAPTER 36

FROM MY HIDING SPOT across the street, I kept my eyes fixed on the library. "Come on, Boyd," I whispered.

At three o'clock exactly, the yellow door opened and the strange little librarian walked out—alone! A moment later Boyd appeared in the window, motioning for me to hurry. I jumped up and ran across the street. It was working.

Boyd met me at the door, grabbed my arm and pulled me to the back of the library. "Here," he said, "your hiding place." We were standing in front of a large, cabinet-type bookcase. The bottom shelf had been emptied. "Get in," he said. "I'm going to build a wall of books in front of you."

I dropped to my hands and knees and crawled into the dark, dusty space. "Okay," I said. "Perfect." I rolled to my side and propped my head in the crook of my arm, watching Boyd's face as he worked quickly to replace the books. "Thanks, Boyd," I said gratefully. "For helping me like this."

Like my words had broken some kind of spell he'd been under, Boyd stopped lining up the books. He sat back on his heels and crossed his arms over his chest. I noticed that his bottom lip was trembling.

"What?" I said. "Why did you stop?"

Boyd said slowly, "It just hit me, what I'm doing. If Mr. Librarian finds out, he might never let me back in the library. I might never get to read another Ratt book."

"Yeah, but he won't find out." I waited, but Boyd didn't answer. I cleared my throat. "So, I think you'd better hurry."

Boyd didn't seem to hear. He continued to sit on his heels, looking straight ahead at something I couldn't see. "I thought this was a good idea. You know, when we were walking on the road together. But now I think it's wrong."

"What do you mean?"

"It's like a betrayal."

"Oh," I said. Sophie's giant alarm clock was ticking in my head, ready to alert the whole world, but I managed to keep my voice calm and steady. "A betrayal to who?" And when he didn't answer I pressed, "To who, Boyd? To Mr. Librarian? To the Ratt? Or, wait—maybe the Drowning Ghost?" My voice was no longer steady—it was higher than I'd ever heard it and shaking, too. I knew the librarian would be back in just a few minutes. Tick, tick, tick.

Still, I tried to hide the anger that was rising up in my chest. "Listen," I said, "someone is hiding something from me. Something about my dad. Don't you think I have a right to know what really happened? Don't you think it's my right?"

"But you had the answer," Boyd said. "It was in *Ratt Volume 1*—"

That was it. My throat started to burn and the feeling in my chest exploded. "That wasn't the answer, Boyd! It was just some made-up story. Yes, my dad did drown. But you're talking like a comic book is real. I'm never going to find anything real in one of your stupid books, Boyd. I can't even believe you think I could!"

I knew I should stop, but the words that came out next were like someone else was speaking them. Some vicious, mean person who'd been raised by wild pigs. "Why do you care so much, anyway? Why have you so completely bought into a comic book world that you won't even go out in your dad's new speedboat? You spend every day after school in this stupid library. You don't have any friends, do you? You think a comic book freak is your friend and you're happy when he includes you in one of his stupid little stories—even if you're just getting chewed alive. Don't you know how sick that is? Don't you know that's weird?"

I wasn't just talking to Boyd anymore. I was talking to Margaret, the girl who clips articles of killer bees. Margaret, who eats her lunch in the bathroom stall.

Boyd didn't answer. Slowly, carefully, he picked up a book and placed it on the shelf. Then he picked up another and another and another. His face was red and I noticed a thin line of sweat above his lip. But he didn't say a word or even look at me. He just kept stacking books until I was almost completely hidden.

I took a deep breath. The words I'd just said were already starting to replay in my head—and already I wanted to take them back. "Boyd—" I started.

But he didn't let me finish. "Mr. Librarian will lock up around seven. Find what you need before the moon gets too high."

"Why?" I asked. "What about the moon?"

Without looking at me, he shoved the last few books onto the shelf, leaving about a quarter inch for a tiny bit of light and some fresh air. Then he answered, "It's a full moon tonight. The Drowning Ghost and Ratt will both be out. Even if you're not on the water, it's a dangerous night. That's why." The words sounded like they'd been forced out of him.

A moment later I heard the bells jingle and, after a few muffled words between Boyd and Mr. Librarian, the bells jingled once again. Boyd had gone.

In the dark dusty tomb of a bookshelf I lay perfectly still, knowing that a cough or a sneeze or even a loud breath might give me away. Nothing left to do but wait, I said to myself. Wait for Mr. Librarian to leave so I could see if those scrapbooks of his really did have the story I had come here to find. After the terrible things I had just said to Boyd, anything else I may have found on the island—like maybe a friend— was probably gone.

CHAPTER 37

BOYD STOOD WAITING FOR the sports bus. Usually this was one of his favorite times of the day—he'd have a new Ratt volume in his backpack and could look forward to reading it on the ride home. But today wasn't the same.

What had started out as one of the very best days of his life now felt pretty close to the worst. He'd thought he had a friend, someone he could talk to and trust. He'd shown her his Ratt collection and shared his most treasured stories. He'd stood up to the Threes for her—and she'd called him stupid, sick, weird. She'd told him to grow up.

Boyd felt something brush up against him. Just as he was about to turn around, a voice stopped him cold. "So you thought you'd be safe on the bus?" Boyd didn't have to look to know who it was. He glanced down at his watch—the bus would be there any moment.

One, Two, and Three circled around and stood close. "Don't worry," said Three. "We'll make sure you get home today." One didn't say a word, just snapped the thin, nylon rope he held in his hands.

Even as Boyd turned to run, he knew it was too late. Four beefy arms grabbed and held him tightly in place.

"See, we spent all afternoon trying to think of the perfect punishment for your crime. We know you don't go swimming because you're afraid of water. We know you don't even go out on your dad's fancy new boat. So after a lot of thoughtful discussion, we came up with the perfect plan." One paused. Two and Three laughed.

Boyd said, "Why don't you just beat me up and get it over with." *Hurry, bus. Hurry, hurry.*

"Because," said One, "beating you up is not the perfect plan. Now, when the bus comes, we're all going to sit together nicely and enjoy the ride home. But before that, you need to call your mom and tell her you won't be coming home tonight. You're spending the night at a friend's."

CHAPTER 38

JUST AS BOYD HAD said he would, Mr. Librarian left his library at seven o'clock. After I heard the jingle of bells, I waited a few moments, then pushed through Boyd's wall of books and crawled out onto the floor. It was a relief to finally have something else to think about—something other than my cramped legs and the last look I'd seen on Boyd's face.

The room was dark except for a small desk lamp that gave off a strange, green glow. I pushed Mr. Librarian's chair in front of the tall shelves filled with scrapbooks, glanced at the titles and decided to start with MURDER. Like climbing the mansion's dark stairway the night before—if something was there, it was better to know right away.

I stepped off the chair and sat down, pushed the box of cherry-filled donuts to the side of the desk and huddled close to the green lamp.

Now, I won't try and get you all riled up with anticipation. The truth is, MURDER was nothing. MURDER was a collection of articles about a string of mysterious cat deaths that occurred on the island like fifteen years ago. The killer, it was eventually discovered, was an extra large raccoon.

DEATH was a letdown, too: a long, handwritten list of all the people who were buried in the island's cemetery. I slumped back in the chair and dropped my head in my hands. I'd been so sure the scrapbooks would help me that now my whole body felt heavy with disappointment.

I thought back to my first few steps off the ferry, just one day ago. I had taken the first step, and the second, and the third. But now I was stuck. I couldn't go back to the mansion and I couldn't go back to Boyd's house after what I'd said to him. Where was Fate now? What was I supposed to do next?

I stepped onto the chair with MURDER and DEATH, trying to remember where they'd been in that long line of scrapbooks. Somewhere around BIRTHS, MARRIAGES AND DIVORCES, CURRENT EVENTS, SPORTS—I stopped. My father had won a medal as a high school swimmer. It was a longshot, but there might be something.

I pulled the scrapbook from the shelf and sat back down at the desk. As soon as I opened the cover, I knew I'd found it.

LOCAL BOY HEADING FOR GOLD

It was the title of an article about my father's dream to become an Olympic swimmer. It listed all his high school records and had a photograph of him with a medal around his neck.

I felt tears running down my face. *There you are, Dad. A champion.* He was just out of the pool, dripping wet and grinning, surrounded by a group of cheering fans. Even on faded newsprint, he was alive and real.

I looked at the photograph again—it was exactly

the same as the drawing in Boyd's comic. Yes, there was my father, just a few years older than I was now. Did I look like him? I couldn't tell. I read the caption underneath:

A champion surrounded by adoring fans, including his biggest fan of all—younger brother (far right).

My eyes froze on the sentence. A younger brother? That meant I had an uncle somewhere. An uncle! I brought the photograph close to my face and squinted down at the boy on the far right. He was standing a little apart from the crowd, but staring at my father with a look of pure joy and adoration. I knew that look. It was one Sophie sometimes gave me.

What was it about that face? I closed my eyes, trying to remember where I'd seen it before. It must have been from a photograph—but how could it have been? I'd never even known I had an uncle. I opened my eyes and took another look at my newly found relative. And that's when it started. The creepy feeling in my belly.

What was it about this face that made my stomach turn? Was it that the eyes were set just a little too close, or was it the way the mouth and chin came together in a skinny little point? The boy looked like a—

I stopped myself.

It couldn't be.

But it was.

This was the same face Boyd had shown me the night before. This was the real-life face of the comic book boy who had turned into a rat. This was my father's brother. This was my uncle. This was the Ratt.

Once there were two boys, about our age. They were best of friends—you could call them brothers, actually, and they did everything together.

Until one started turning into a rat.

I thought about the movement in the upstairs window, that very first day. That must have been him. He must have been hiding in that house, undetected, all these years, collecting garbage and churning out strange little books. *Dad's crazy side of the family.*

I thought about the comic he'd sent Lizzie, post-marked right after my dad died. Had he been trying to tell her what had happened? How my dad had died? Had Boyd been right all along?

I stood up quickly. My hands were sweaty and my head felt dizzy. I knew where I had to go. Back for the comic. Back to the mansion. Even in the dark, even all alone. It was the only way.

I'm not sure if I heard the sound first or saw the movement, but right as I was stepping away from the desk, I knew that I was no longer alone—someone was just outside the library door.

I froze. I panicked. I fumbled with the scrapbook and it fell to the floor. Quickly, I dropped to my knees and slid underneath the desk. The door creaked open so slowly that the bells barely made a sound. I held my breath. Maybe it was Boyd. Or Mr. Librarian coming back for the box of cherry-filled donuts he'd left, untouched, on the desk.

Scratch, scratch, sniff.

Boyd didn't make a sound like that when he walked.

Scratch, scratch, sniff.

Or Mr. Librarian, either. I closed my eyes. *I am not here. I am home in bed. Wake up now.*

The footsteps stopped. I opened my eyes to six feet, only inches from my face. Two were extra large and wrapped in scraps of leather and mismatched bits of twine. The other four were very small, had long sharp nails, and were covered with dirty, matted fur.

"*Grrrr.*" Two suspicious eyes glared at me from underneath the desk. "*Grrrr.*" It was the strangest looking dog I'd ever seen, with teeth too long to fit in its mouth. I pulled my knees to my chest and made myself as small as possible. "*Grrrr.*" Eyes and teeth, moving closer.

"Leave it," a voice whispered, and the dog blinked its watery, bulging eyes. A human voice? If it was, it was like no human voice I'd ever heard. High-pitched and breathless, this voice sounded like it was rarely used. A cherry-filled donut dropped on the floor in front of me and the angry little beast attacked it with furor—his eyes never leaving my face.

I watched the two large feet in their odd leather wrappings move quietly around the desk and stop when they came upon the scrapbook I'd dropped. Then I heard a long, high release of breath as a hand reached down to the floor. Until that moment, I'd laughed at Boyd for believing that a human being could really, truly turn into a rat. But when I saw the hand, I wasn't so sure anymore.

This hand—it was like a human hand, only not. It had long, thin fingers with thick, yellow nails, so pointy they looked sharp. And there was hair. Not normal hair that some grown-ups have on their knuckles—this hair was more like fur.

I watched the hand flip open the scrapbook. I watched the long, thin finger trace the outline of my father's photograph. Then, suddenly, the scrapbook was lifted off the floor and out of my sight. A moment later there was a shuffle of footsteps, a whimper from the dog, and a click of the library door. Then silence.

Was it a trick? Would he wait fifteen seconds, then open the door to catch me sneaking out from underneath the desk? Should I stay where I was or make a run for it? What would Tina Louise do? I tried to ask her, but it was no use. She was back home, sitting at the kitchen table doing her math homework. She was safe.

The only thing I could do was take a chance. I crawled out from underneath the desk, ready to make a dash for the door. I would run to the spot where I'd hidden Boyd's bike, ride it back to his house and tell him—I stopped. Tell him what? Tell him about the fingers?

The library was dark and empty. I looked down at the scrapbook, now on the librarian's chair, and thought of the hairy hand, rifling through the pages, the sharp intake of breath when he'd come across the article about my father.

I picked up the scrapbook and opened the cover. The article didn't have the answer I was looking for, but it was something to hold onto, something to take back with me. I turned the page. I turned another. I kept turning pages even after I knew for certain—the article was gone.

I glanced around the floor, the desk. The entire box of donuts—it was gone, too. And on the desk, right where the donuts had been, was a new Ratt book, opened to a page in the middle.

It took me a moment to realize what I was looking at. I picked it up and held it close to my face. "No," I whispered. *Oh, no.*

There was Boyd, bound and gagged and tied to the control panel of a small motorboat. On the next page was a map with arrows that pointed the way to a boathouse on the beach.

Maybe this was just a warning, like the one left on Boyd's front porch. Maybe Boyd was safe in his house, doing the dishes, emptying the garbage, reading a book. I tried to imagine all the normal things Boyd could be doing, but I didn't believe any of them. Maybe it was because I'd seen the long fingers and hairy hand that made this warning seem different; this one seemed horribly real.

Heart pounding in my chest, I ran out of the library and into the dark, empty street—down to the alley where I'd stashed Boyd's bike. "Hold on," I whispered, grabbing the handlebars and jumping on. *Hold on, Boyd, I'm coming.*

CHAPTER 39

EVEN THOUGH THE NIGHT was quiet and the waves lapping up against the side of the boat were gentle, still they made it rock and shake. And Boyd, tied to the steering wheel of his dad's new motorboat, cringed with every slight movement. Earlier he'd cried—muffled sobs that had soaked the bandanna stuffed into his mouth. Now his face was raw and itchy with salt, both from the spray of the waves and his tears.

"If I get out of this, Dad, I promise I'll go out on this boat with you." Boyd had made several vows that night—all the ways he would change his life if he survived the night. He would eat his rice and seaweed gratefully. Tell his mom he loved her and stop reading comics during math. Try harder at team sports and maybe even become pen pals with a prisoner. With each vow he'd felt a small bit of hope for a promising future.

Except for this last one. Even as the muffled words left his tongue and lodged themselves between the folds of the hankie, he knew he was lying. He wouldn't go out on this boat with his dad. Not ever. If he made it out of this boathouse alive, he'd stay as far away from the water as possible. Full moon or not. Forever. And when he grew up he'd move to a place like Arizona or New Mexico—a nice, safe place surrounded by bone-dry land.

Another wave sent the little boat rocking. Boyd hung his head and willed his stomach to stay calm. There was no way his parents would find him that night—they wouldn't even come looking. ("Of course you can spend the night at a friend's house," his mother had said too eagerly on the phone. *Her son had a friend! A friend!*) The Threes had laughed as they tied him up. "Maybe your rat man will help you out of this one," they said.

Boyd hadn't answered. He knew his only hope was Margaret, and she wasn't any hope at all, really. She was probably still mad at him for being such a geek, and even if she wasn't, there's no way she'd ever find him—a boathouse on the night of a full moon was the last place anyone would come looking for someone like him.

CHAPTER 40

BY THE TIME I SPOTTED Boyd's porch light, I was dripping with sweat. The ride through the trees had been dark and spooky, but as soon as I'd reached the water the moon had stayed with me the rest of the way.

I pumped my aching legs the last hundred yards to Boyd's house, then dropped the bike on the front lawn and started to run. The comic was crammed in my back pocket, but I didn't need to look at it to know where to go. Down to the beach and along the coast—it was like the map had branded itself on my brain.

Down to the water I ran. Was it really only last Sunday I'd run through this very field for the first time?

When I got to the beach, the tide was low. I kept to the jagged shoreline, following a hand-drawn arrow that only I could see, grateful to the moon for lighting the way.

"Boyd?" I called his name as I stumbled over slippery rocks. Straight ahead, just a few hundred yards in front of me, was what looked like a very small house. The boathouse. For the first time since leaving the library, I let myself ask the question: Is this a trap?

Why else would the Ratt leave a map—*a map!*—showing where Boyd would be? And would Boyd really even be there? Or was I heading into a face-to-face showdown with my long-lost uncle?

The smart thing would have been to turn around and run back to Boyd's house. Knock on the door and say to the grown-up who opened it, "I think your son might be in trouble."

But I didn't. The ride I was on was spinning so fast, I had no idea how to step off. So instead, when I reached the side of the wooden boathouse, I looked for the small door with the rusted knob. Just like in the comic.

Turn, I told my shaking hand. Don't think of the hairy fingers or the army of rats or the Drowning Ghost or the fact that your uncle is a rodent. Just think about Boyd. Just turn the knob and push.

CHAPTER 41

BOYD THOUGHT ABOUT the Drowning Ghost and the big, gaping holes where the crabs had eaten out his eyes. Then he closed his own and, just for a moment, tried to imagine what life would be like without them.

When he opened them again, the boathouse door was ajar and a ghostly figure stood glowing in a small patch of moonlight. Boyd tried to scream but the soggy bandanna made him gag. Then the ghostly figure said his name and was suddenly no longer ghostly. It was Margaret.

CHAPTER 42

IT TOOK A MOMENT to make out that the small figure huddled in the middle of the boat was really Boyd. I shouted his name, then didn't know what to say after that, so I just shouted his name again, and then tried to figure out how to get him off the boat.

A boathouse is like a garage, except where the concrete floor should be, there is water. And where the garage door should be, there is nothing—nothing stopping the boat from floating out into wide-open water but a piece of heavy rope and a hook.

A narrow wooden walkway flanked the length of the boat. One careless move on the wet planks and I could have slipped into the dark water below, so I stepped slowly and carefully. "How do I get on?" I asked, looking across the strip of water.

Through his bandanna, Boyd said something that sounded like, "Jump!" and then, "Be careful." I took a deep breath and jumped. The next thing I knew I was on the bottom of the boat, looking up into Boyd's grateful eyes. I'd made it.

I reached over and pulled the soggy bandanna from his mouth. "How did you know—" he sputtered and choked. "How did you know I was here?" I started working on the knot that held his hands to the steering wheel. "Margaret," he asked again, "how did you know?"

As the knot came undone in my hands, I glanced over my shoulder, but no glittering eyes watched us from the corner. "We'd better get out of here," I said.

Boyd scrambled to the edge of the boat and leaped across to the walkway. He turned to me and held out his hand, shivering from hours in the damp air. "It's really not far," he said reassuringly. "Like jumping over a mud puddle."

I nodded, reached for his outstretched hand and jumped. Almost instantly, I felt Boyd's fingers wrap around my wrist, holding me steady on the slippery wooden plank. "Thanks," I said. He nodded, dropped my wrist and turned away. I followed him along the walkway to the small side door. When we stepped out of the boathouse, the air seemed colder.

All night I'd had this feeling—it was like I'd been stepping in and out of different worlds. And all the worlds were somehow connected, but also completely separate. I was the only thing that linked them to-gether. Now, as I followed Boyd away from the boat-house, I realized I'd just slipped into a new one again.

Boyd didn't follow the beach trail. Glancing at the full moon, he turned toward the field. "Let's stay away from the water," he said.

I followed, thinking of a way to explain all the dif-ferent worlds to him. "Boyd," I started, but I couldn't finish. *I know who the Ratt really is. I saw his hands.* Instead, I pulled the comic from my back pocket and held it out. "Look," I said.

Boyd stopped and turned. He looked down at the book, then up at me. "Open it," I said.

Boyd took the book and opened to the first page. There, under the light of the moon, he saw himself being abducted by Ratt. He saw the rope being tied around his hands and the bandanna being shoved into his mouth. "Now you'll be in hands worse than my own," Ratt hissed.

Boyd shook his head slowly. "I don't believe it," he said. "I don't believe it."

"That's how I knew where to find you. See the map?"

"He must have known you were in the library. And that you would come to save me." Boyd looked up at me. His eyes were shining.

"I know. I thought it would be a trap. But here we are, not trapped. Not yet, anyway."

"I don't believe it," Boyd said again.

"I know." Right then is when I should have said the rest. What I saw in the library. But I couldn't. The truth was, I was scared. If the Ratt was my uncle, what did that make me?

CHAPTER 43

Editor's Note:

I think it would be a good time to peek back in on Sophie. By now, she's probably sitting along the side of Waterfront Road, resting her small, weary feet. It's probably dark, and she's probably scared with those strange rustling noises in the woods all around her. As she fights back the tears and wonders if she'll ever see her big sister again, she hears another kind of noise, a more civilized and familiar one. Let's say Sophie hears a car. No, wait—even better. A minivan. Let's say blue.

At this point Sophie is so tired she doesn't bother to hide behind a tree. And when the blue minivan slows to a stop and a concerned, kindly face peers out from the driver's-side window, Sophie is relieved. She glances to the backseat and sees a chubby toddler—no, two! twins!—strapped securely to their five-point harness car seats.

"Are you okay?" asks the minivan mom. "Do you need a ride?"

Without a word or even a nod, Sophie picks up her suitcase and walks around to the passenger side of the van. "Let me help you with that," says the kindly minivan mom, opening the door and grabbing the handle of the suitcase.

Or something like that.

CHAPTER 44

CHAPTER 45

BOYD CLEARED HIS THROAT. As soon as Margaret had pulled the bandanna from his mouth, he'd wanted to tell her everything—how the Threes had abducted him; about the cell-phone call to his mother and the bus ride home. But it had taken him a while to put the words together and, by the time he was ready, it was too late. The moment he'd seen himself in the pages of the new Ratt book, it was too late.

Soon you'll be in hands worse than my own, Ratt had said as he'd tied Boyd's hands to the motorboat. That was so much better than being dragged down the beach by the three biggest idiots on the island.

"I still don't get it," Margaret said. "Why would he draw a map to show where you were if it wasn't a trap?" The two were huddled in the middle of the big field next to the mansion. They'd already decided that Margaret would go back for the first comic, and now they were waiting for the moon to tell them when it was time.

Boyd cleared his throat again. "Well," he said, "maybe he felt his territory was being threatened. I mean, you put up a For Sale sign, after all."

Margaret shook her head slowly. "You're still defending him, Boyd. After what he did to you, he's still your hero. No offense, but if you're going to have a hero, why not someone like Superman?"

Boyd suddenly remembered her words in the library—every single one. He felt the same pressure on his chest and the sick taste in his throat—the one that made him want to get up and run and hide away forever. So why couldn't he do it? Was he even too afraid to run? He looked down at his fingers. "It's easy for you, isn't it? You're pretty. You have friends."

Margaret didn't answer at first. Then she said, "What does that have to do with anything?"

"It's easy to like Superman, that's what. What's not to like? Even his name: Super Man." Boyd stopped. Why bother? "You wouldn't understand," he said.

"Boyd—" Margaret started. She cleared her throat. "What?"

"Nothing," she said. "Let's just go over the plan again."

CHAPTER 46

WE CALLED IT "THE PLAN" like it involved tiny cameras installed in X-ray glasses and microphones implanted behind our ears. But really it was nothing like that. The plan was simply that I would sneak back into the house and retrieve my backpack with *Ratt Volume 1*. Calling it "the plan" made it seem safe and solid—two things it was not.

I looked up at the moon. Somehow it seemed warm on my face. "Is it time?" I asked.

Boyd angled his hand against the sky. "No," he said. "Not yet. When the moon is directly over that small window in the back. That's when he leaves to battle the Drowning Ghost."

I shuddered, thinking about going back into that dark house, all alone. "And you're sure he'll be gone?"

"I'm sure," Boyd said. "On nights when the moon is full, he goes out twice. Once to scavenge and once to battle."

I tilted my head back and closed my eyes. Yes, I knew why he went out the first time. I'd been there. But what did it mean to battle the Drowning Ghost? How did that translate in this world?

I heard Boyd next to me, rustling the pages of the comic. Even with his little speech about Superman, I still couldn't understand how he could so easily forget what Ratt had done to him.

Of course, after all the terrible things I'd said to him in the library, I was surprised he was sitting next to me, too. My face burned when I remembered the words that had shot out of my mouth. And Boyd had said I was pretty; he thought I had friends back home. How funny.

I opened my eyes. Boyd was still holding the comic, but he was staring at my face. He quickly looked away, flustered, like I'd caught him doing something wrong. "I'm really sorry for what I said in the library," I said.

Boyd looked down at the comic. "Don't worry about it," he mumbled.

I knew sorry wasn't enough. "Boyd," I said quickly, trying to get it out before I had a chance to change my mind. "I eat my lunch in the bathroom stall."

Boyd continued to stare at the comic, but I watched his eyes blink rapidly, trying to comprehend. "What?"

"At school. Every day. So I don't have to go to the lunchroom."

"You do?"

"Yes." I remembered the girls peeking over the stall, seeing me standing there with my pepperoni pizza. *Gross.*

"Well," Boyd said finally. "Maybe you should try the library." He glanced at me and smiled shyly.

"Yeah," I said, "that's a good idea." I met his eyes and smiled back.

CHAPTER 47

CHAPTER 48

THERE'S THAT MOMENT, right before you blow out the candles on your birthday cake, that moment you have a fleeting sense of something not so happy and not so birthday. Maybe it comes from understanding the order of things, because I know Sophie doesn't feel it yet. When I was her age, I didn't feel it, either. But once you understand the order of things, you know that when the presents are opened, you'll never again be able to wonder what they might be. And when the candles are blown out, it's time to eat the cake. And when the cake is eaten, there's nothing left but to say thank you and send everyone home.

I still like cake and I still like presents. It's just that now, there's one little moment of sadness right before I blow out the candles—that one little moment where I peek into the future and say good-bye to another birthday, even before it's over.

"What are you thinking about?"

Boyd's loud whisper startled me out of remembering my last birthday cake, which had been a boy on a rocket ship—the only decorated cake left in the supermarket on Bare Minimum for Survival Day. "I was thinking about birthdays," I whispered back. We were sitting cross-legged in the field next to the mansion. The ground was cold and hard. We'd been out there for nearly an hour, waiting for the moon to hit the house at the exact right angle.

"What about birthdays?"

"Birthday cake," I answered. The nice woman in the supermarket bakery had written "Happy 12th, Margaret," in green frosting that matched the rocket ship, then added some green strands to the boy's head to make it look like my shoulder-length hair. Lizzie and Sophie had both laughed.

"Does this mean that when you're twelve, your hair will turn green?" asked Sophie, trying to be cute.

"Let's hope not," said Lizzie, trying to be a mom.

"You just wait," I said to them both. *You just wait and see what twelve means.*

And now, lying in that field next to Boyd, I knew why I had ended up with that cake. Twelve wasn't the bright green hair—it was the rocket ship, taking me to a place I could never have imagined.

"I was thinking about when you eat your cake, it means your birthday is about to end," I said. "Like tonight. Tonight when we find the book, we'll know about my dad and my—" I stopped myself quickly. I'd told him about eating my lunch in the bathroom stall. About the Chihuahuas and killer bees and being sent to three different schools in one year. But I couldn't tell him what I'd discovered about the Ratt. I couldn't say it out loud.

How funny, that we both wanted the same thing. I wanted to know the truth about my dad, and Boyd wanted to know how the Drowning Ghost came to be. How funny that we had somehow managed to find each other.

"Not funny—it's Fate," Tina Louise hissed at me from behind a bush.

"Right," I whispered back.

"What?" asked Boyd.

I shook my head. "Nothing." I turned away so he wouldn't see how scared I was. A moment later I felt his hand touch my shirt and when I turned back, his face was only inches away from mine. Besides my mom and my sister, I'd never been that close to anyone before. I tried to swallow, but my throat wouldn't let me.

"Margaret—" he said, moving his other arm a little closer. The whole world froze.

"What?" My heart was pounding some sort of crazy SOS signal, and a girl with green hair was looking down at me from a rocket ship and laughing.

"The moon. Look. It's time."

I looked up at the moon. Somehow it had snuck over to the other side of the house and was now shining into the last room on the upstairs floor. "Okay," I said, swallowing hard. So this wasn't the movies and I wasn't about to kiss a boy in the middle of a field, underneath a full moon. I was Margaret, after all. Margaret who ate her lunch in a bathroom stall and worried about dogs the size of cats. Margaret, the girl with a rodent for an uncle.

"I still think I should come with you," he said.

I shook my head. "I'm just going to run in and find my backpack. You need to be here in case anything goes wrong."

"Don't forget the flashlight."

"Right," I said. "I'm pretty sure it dropped at the bottom of the stairs. As soon as I find it, I'll shine it through the window to let you know I'm okay. If I can't find it, I'll come back out."

"Right," said Boyd. "I'll wait for you. I won't take my eyes off the window."

"Okay."

Boyd started mumbling to himself, listing all the things that could go wrong. "I'll get my dad and if my dad doesn't believe me, I'll call the police—"

I cut him off. "I guess I shouldn't waste any more time."

Boyd nodded and glanced back at the moon. I got to my feet, crouched low and started toward the mansion.

"See you, Margaret," he whispered. His voice was shaking.

Slowly, I made my way to the mansion. Was the Ratt out in the field, too, watching me creep to his home? Had he been watching us this whole time, also waiting for this moment? "Don't think," I told myself, like I did when I first walked off the ferry. "Just step."

I stood on the front porch and thought about the night before—the footsteps chasing me and the door that wouldn't open. This time, when I put the key in the lock, the knob turned easily in my hand. I pushed the door open and stepped inside.

Once again the moon showed me the way to the bottom of the stairs and, just as I'd thought, there was my flashlight. I picked it up and turned it on—it worked! Quickly, I made my way to one of the boarded-up windows and shone the light through a large crack. I waved it wildly, up and down. *Here I am, Boyd. I made it!* Then I swung the flashlight around in the direction of the stairway. *Hurry, hurry, hurry.*

With the flashlight leading the way, I ran up the steps to the first landing. Then the next. I stood at the top of the stairs and shone the light into the cavelike darkness. The three doors that I'd opened the night before were closed again. I ran the flashlight along the floor, stopping in front of the third door on the left. There was my backpack on the floor, right where I had thrown it. Quietly, I crept over to it, knelt down and pulled out the package. But something was wrong, I could tell right away. Hands trembling, I opened the flap and looked inside. Even before I saw what was missing, I knew. The comic book was gone.

I could either run back to the field and tell Boyd that the book was gone, or I could stay where I was and try to find it. Since neither option was very good, I tried to imagine myself in the future, thinking back to this very moment. *My hair is pulled back in a tight, gray bun. I'm wearing a long, white night-*

gown and my spindly hands pull the bed covers up around my neck because my frail bones are chilled. All I can think about is the mystery of my father's death, which has haunted me my entire life. "If only, if only," I mumble to myself.

That was all it took. "Okay," I whispered. "Okay." I took one step, then another. I was floating, I was dreaming, I was in a movie with a spooky soundtrack. I somehow took enough steps to get me down the dark hallway, past the three closed doors. I took a few more and found myself in front of the fourth—the only one I hadn't gone into the night before. And, unlike the other three, this door was open. Just a crack, but it was open enough to let a thin sliver of moonlight shine through.

Was this a sign? Or was it the trap? I waited for an answer, but none came. "What now?" I asked myself.

"Step," answered the gray-haired Margaret clutching her nightie to her shrunken chest. "Step, step." Very slowly, very quietly, I pushed open the fourth door on the right.

If I had seen this room the night before, I wouldn't have understood. But now as I stood in the doorway, I wanted to cry.

This was not a junk drawer. It was not a workshop or a painter's studio. This was a bedroom—a boy's bedroom, in perfect time-capsuled order. On each side of the room was a twin bed with matching bedspreads. Over each bed was a wooden shelf, one cluttered with seashells and driftwood and shiny rocks; the other with gleaming trophies and medals. Swimming medals.

This was the bedroom my father grew up in—one of those beds was his. And the other? The other was where my uncle had probably spent hours doodling and daydreaming about junkyards and garbage cans and rotting cheese.

Across from me was a large, rectangular window; underneath the window was a small, tidy desk with a matching wooden chair. The moon was directly outside the window, flooding the room with light and watching over me like a wise, old friend. *Come here*, it seemed to say. *Closer.*

I took a step, and that's when I saw it—the book on the desk, almost like it had been waiting for me. I shivered suddenly, wondering if the Ratt had anticipated my every move. He'd set a trap, hadn't he? Just like he did with Boyd in the boathouse, he'd set a trap and I'd sniffed my way into the heart of it. What would I do next, Uncle Ratt? Would I grab the book and run? And are you here watching me?

I glanced at the dark corners of the room. As scared as I was, I knew one thing for certain: he wanted me to read the book, just as he'd wanted Lizzie to read it years before. I took a step closer. I pulled the chair out from the desk. "What are you doing?" the moon asked softly. "You could go get your friend in the field. You could take the book with you."

But I knew, as I sat down in the small wooden

chair and opened the cover of *Ratt Volume 1: How to Disappear Completely and Never Be Found*—I knew I had to read it alone.

The pictures were familiar, but for the first time I was really seeing them. There was my father and his brother, all grown up. My father had come back for him, to take him off the island, but first they decided to go out in the small canoe, one last time. As I read the words, the pictures began to move in front of me. I watched two men grab a canoe and carry it down to the water. I heard their feet on the wooden dock and the soft lapping of waves. I didn't have to look at the pictures anymore to see the two men who, suddenly, seemed like two boys. They were moving right in front of me.

One night two friends went swimming. It was summer and the moon was full. The two friends hadn't seen each other in a long, long time. They went swimming from a canoe, just like they used to do on summer nights when they were boys together. The canoe let them go out, way out, to where the water was so deep and dark, they were almost afraid.

Together they slipped over the side of the canoe. Being in the water was like being home. One leaned back and let the water wrap around him like a blanket. And he looked up, into the sky. A million stars lifted him up to the moon, which was so bright on his face it made him warm. And he knew right then, if he stayed with the stars and the moon and the water, he would be happy.

So he closed his eyes and felt the water cover his face, and it was so soft, like a blanket, and the moon kept him warm. And he said, "The water is pulling me down. It wants me to stay."

And the other one got scared and said, "Don't let it." And he reached over. And he tried to stop it, he tried to pull his friend up. And they fought—right there in the deep, dark water. Stupid, really, because what happened after that was the water turned on them both. It was no longer a warm blanket— it was cold and desperate and hungry. The moon, even the moon lost its warmth when it saw what was happening. Maybe they planned it together, the moon and the water, maybe they planned it so they could keep one of them forever. Because that's what happened. They kept one for themselves.

The one they kept they named the Drowning Ghost. And once a month, when the moon is full, he rises from the bottom of the sea. His face, once handsome and smooth, is now bloated white, and his skin peels off in long, ragged strips. Tiny crabs have eaten out

*his eyes and now make their home in the
large, empty sockets.*

*Once a month, when the moon is full, he
sneaks up behind an unsuspecting boater
or fisherman. Their only warning is a long,
slow chill down the back of their neck—the
icy finger of the Drowning Ghost. Down,
down, down to the bottom of the sea where
he will scoop out their eyes for his own.*

When I finished, I held the book to my chest and
closed my eyes. I wanted to cry, not because of all the
sad little words that made up the story, but because I
still didn't know what really happened. I knew they
went out on the water and that one had wanted to stay,
had wanted the water to pull him down. But was it my
father?

I opened my eyes and looked out at the water, so
peaceful and still. A lone canoe with two figures moved
slowly but steadily away from shore. I shuddered, thinking of that other canoe, all those years before, carrying
my father and uncle to their brief, tragic reunion. And
then my uncle, hiding out here alone.

I thought about Lizzie at home with two children,
waiting for her husband to return. And when he didn't,
spending the next four years hiding out, too.

Didn't they know this wasn't just their story?
Didn't they know that it was mine? And Sophie's? And
by keeping it secret, she made me keep it secret, too?

Made me feel there was a reason to feel ashamed, a reason to hide.

Suddenly, I knew one thing for certain. I didn't want to be like them. I didn't want to hide anymore. I wanted to find Boyd. I wanted to find Boyd and tell him everything, including who Ratt really was. And the Drowning Ghost, too.

When I grabbed *Ratt Volume 1*, a sheet of paper slipped loose and drifted down to the floor. I picked it up and held it to the moonlight. It was another one-page Ratt story, similar to the warning left on Boyd's doorstep. This one showed Ratt in his bedroom with a young girl. *I'm looking for my sister,* she is saying. *Will you take me to my sister now?*

The hairs on my arms and the back of my neck realized what I was looking at a moment before my brain did. They stood straight up and shrieked her name. "Sophie!" I grabbed the flashlight and swung it around the room. "Sophie!" She couldn't really be here—I'd spoken to her on the phone just that morning. At the foot of one of the twin beds was a small suitcase. I moved closer. Was it one from the hall closet back home? My hands started to shake as I yanked down the zipper. I reached in and pulled out the first thing my fingers touched: a tiny piece to THE HARDEST JIGSAW EVER MADE.

Yes. But first, would you like to see my boat?

"Sophie!" I screamed, dropping the book, the

drawing, the flashlight. I rushed out the door and stumbled blindly through the dark hallway. "Sophie!" I screamed again, even though I knew I was the only one in the house.

So this was his trap! He wanted me to know he had her. He wanted me to know he had her with him, out in a canoe. Of course! That's why Ratt had tied Boyd up and then sent me to save him—it got us both out of the way so he could take Sophie.

But why? Why Sophie? What could he possibly want from her?

I made it to the top of the stairs and began feeling my way down. *Sophie, Sophie, Sophie,* I whispered. *I'm coming for you.* When I got to the first landing, I heard the growl. This time I didn't care—not even when I felt the sharp teeth sink into my leg. All I could think about was Sophie, my tiny sister out on a boat with the same crazy man who was out with my dad when he drowned.

I made it to the bottom of the stairs, the snarling dog still right at my heels. The moon showed me the way to the front door. Out the door, down the steps, across the yard and through the field.

"Margaret?" It was Boyd, calling my name. "Margaret?"

I heard the heavy breathing of the dog, struggling to keep up with me, and then the pounding of Boyd's feet not far behind. "Margaret, stop! Where are you going? I'll get my dad."

I didn't answer. I couldn't. All I could do was run. I knew exactly where I needed to go, but what I would do once I got there—I had absolutely no idea.

Editor's Note:

I think it would be useful to pause for a moment and think about the moon. Have you ever noticed that the moon can be in several places at one time? Do this experiment on the night of the next full moon: Call up your grandmother who lives in Florida and say, "Gee, Grandma, the moon is right over my head." And if she doesn't say, "Yes, dear, it's over mine, too—isn't it lovely?" I'll refund every penny you spent on this book.

If you don't have a grandmother in Florida, pick up the telephone and dial any number at all— you might reach Maine or Italy or Mississippi. Ask them, "How's the moon over there?" and you'll probably hear, "Lovely," "Bella," and "Reaaaal purdy." (The refund only works for the grandmother in Florida, though.)

I tell you this because the moon that night was working overtime, keeping track of people. As it was lighting the path to the boathouse for Margaret and Boyd, it was also peeking its face through the windshield of a parked car on a ferry boat where a very scared woman sat chewing her fingernails, and, all the while, shining peacefully on a small blue canoe gliding silently across deep, dark waters.

CHAPTER 49

"**MARGARET—I DON'T KNOW** how!" Boyd stood in the doorway of the boathouse, watching Margaret try to bring the small motorboat to life. He wanted to help, he really did, but there was nothing in the world that would get him out on the water, especially the night of a full moon. "Let me get my dad—" he started again, but Margaret wouldn't let him finish.

"No!" she shouted. "It will take too long. He won't believe you. Listen to me. He's got my little sister. He's out there with my sister. I don't know exactly what happened to my dad, but I know he was there. He's crazy, Boyd. Look what he did to you. Please. You have to help me."

Boyd's face went pale. If only he'd told her the truth about the Threes, maybe this wouldn't be happening right now. Could he tell her now? Tell her that he lied? "I don't think he'd hurt her—"

"Boyd! He tied you up! He stuffed a handkerchief in your mouth—"

"Margaret—"

"Just help me get it started," she begged. "Just help me get it started, Boyd. You must have seen your dad do it. You must know how to at least get it started. Please. You don't even have to go out there with me—"

"But you don't even know how to drive it—"

Margaret was crying now. "It's my fault," she said. "If anything happens to her—" She tried to start the engine again, but nothing.

"Okay, Margaret." Boyd heard his voice float out over the water. "Okay." He jumped onto the boat, making it rock back and forth. "You'll need to unhook the rope from the dock." He pushed her away from the steering wheel.

Margaret jumped off the boat like she'd been doing it for years. She ran around to the rope and the hook and waited. "Tell me when."

Boyd's hand was frozen. He should tell her the truth. He should tell her the truth before they got out on the water.

"Now, Boyd? Now?"

"No, not yet," he said. He needed to tell her. He needed to tell her first. From somewhere far away he heard a dog barking. He'd never heard a dog barking out here before.

"Hurry, Boyd."

Boyd turned the key and the engine sputtered to life. "Okay!" he cried. "Unhook the rope!"

Margaret hoisted the rope off the large, metal hook.

"Throw it to me," Boyd called over the sound of the engine. "And get in here, quick."

Margaret threw him the rope, then ran around to the side and jumped back onto the boat. Boyd's hands were wrapped so tightly around the steering wheel that his knuckles were bone white. "Let's go," Margaret said.

Boyd shook his head slowly.

"Boyd!" Margaret shouted over the rumble of the engine. "We have to go!" The air in the boathouse was thick with gas fumes.

"I can't, Margaret. I can't go out there."

Margaret pushed him out of the way. "Then show me what to do. Just show me what to do."

Boyd lowered his head. "You don't understand," he started.

"Please, Boyd," Margaret begged, almost crying now. "Just show me how to drive it. Please. Please." And as she waited for him to respond, the engine started to falter. The engine started to die.

Boyd looked up. Tears were streaming down his face. He couldn't tell her. He couldn't.

He lifted one hand off the steering wheel and took hold of the throttle. "Hold on," he said, giving it a twist. And then they were off.

Editor's Note:

If it weren't for one quiet moment out on the canoe, this story would always have a missing piece, right in the middle. So bear with me, please. Let me tell it as if I were there, even though, of course, I couldn't have been. Trust me on this: I won't tell you anything that didn't happen. A word may be changed here or there, but nothing more. I promise.

Ratt glanced up at the moon, steered to the right, then pulled the paddle into the canoe. He stared down into the water, as if searching for something only he could see. "We're here," he said, and the night seemed to hold its breath.

The gentle rocking of the boat and the soft night air had lulled Sophie into a drowsy spell, but when Ratt spoke, she was suddenly wide awake. "You said Margaret would be here."

"I said she'd come. She'll come." He pointed at the water. "This is where it happened."

"Margaret needs to see it, too."

"He was my big brother just like Margaret is your big brother."

"Margaret's my sister."

"Yes. And I used to wear his medals around my neck."

Sophie reached into her shirt and took out the swimming medal Margaret had given her. She pulled it over her head and offered it to him.

Ratt stared at the medal, then slowly reached out and took it from her hand. He brought it to his mouth, breathed on it and rubbed it against his tattered buckskin sleeve until it shone like new. Slowly, reverently, he draped it around his neck. Then shyly, nervously, he cleared his throat. "I've wanted to show you this place for a long, long time," he said.

Sophie looked around again, expecting to see an island with palm trees or a half-submerged submarine or at least a giant lily pad. Instead, all she saw was water, and Sophie was growing tired of seeing water.

Ratt looked up. He sniffed the air. A change was coming, he could sense it. "Everything is about to change," he said. "And I have very little time to tell you what I need to tell you."

Something about the way he said it made Sophie straighten her shoulders and pay attention. "Okay," she said. "Then tell me."

So Ratt began from the beginning. He told her about her father—how his hair was shiny and bleached golden white from the water and sun. He told her about the junkyard they had discovered and the beautiful objects they created from things other people threw away. He told her about the day he realized he was turning into a rat and how his big brother, trying to be kind, tried to turn himself into a rat, too. "But," he said to Sophie, "you're either a rat or you aren't."

"Am I a rat?"

"No," he said.

"Maybe my sister is part rat."

"Hmmm. Maybe." Ratt glanced over Sophie's head.

"What are you looking at?" Sophie asked, turning around in the boat.

"They're coming. And I must finish before they come."

"Who's coming?"

"Listen. Your father—he came back to get me. Years after he left the island, he came back for me."

"Was I born yet?"

"You were a tiny girl. I knew about you because he sent me your picture. You looked like a mouse. In my head I called you Sophie Mouse."

Sophie looked pleased. "You did?" she asked, liking the sound of it. Sophie Mouse. Two names, like Tina Louise.

"Yes. He came to force me back into civilization, once and for all. But, you see, I knew that would destroy me. A rat cannot live among people. Tell me—what's the one thing humans fear and despise more than anything else?"

"Um," said Sophie. "Um."

"Rats!" exclaimed the Ratt. "Rats!" He picked up the paddle and started to row.

"I thought this was the place we were going to meet Margaret," said Sophie nervously. "How will she find me now?"

"Don't you hear? Don't you hear?"

Sophie closed her eyes and listened. She did hear something. Something like the low rumble of a motor. Of course—it was a boat. Sophie was relieved. Things had been getting a little too strange, even for her. "Mr. Ratt, it's okay," she said. "It's probably just Margaret, coming to meet us."

Ratt glared at her with his odd, piercing eyes. "Listen to me," he said, still paddling furiously. "This is important. This is the only thing that's important. I must finish this before they come."

And then he told her. He told her about the night her father came to bring him back to live in human society. He told her about going out on the boat together for the very last time. He told her the biggest story of his life, the one he'd kept hidden away all those years. He told her everything. And when he was finished, a very strange thing happened. For the first time in her life, Sophie didn't know what to say.

CHAPTER 50

"*SOPHIE!*" *EACH TIME I* called her name the wind seemed to gobble it up and swallow it down. My throat was raw and sore, but I kept calling. It was all I could do.

Boyd shouted something over his shoulder. He seemed to have gotten the hang of driving, and we were flying over the water so fast, I had to hold on to the seat with both hands. "I can't hear you!" I cried.

He turned his head so I could see the side of his mouth, and he shouted it again. "Up ahead—I think I see them."

I scrambled to the front of the boat. "Where? Where are they?"

Boyd unclenched one hand from the steering wheel and pointed to a dark patch on the water. As we moved closer, the dark patch took shape: two figures in a canoe.

"That's her!" I shouted. Sophie, Sophie, Sophie. I wanted to laugh and cry. My little sister—we'd found her!

"What should I do, Margaret? Do you want me to try and get close?"

"Yes," I said. "Get as close as you can so I can talk to him." I sounded more sure than I felt.

It seemed we'd been out on the water for such a long time that, when I glanced back, I was surprised I could still see the shore. How strange, to see the mansion from the water, the lights in the windows making it look like a giant gingerbread house at Christmastime.

I turned back to the canoe—and then I froze. The lights in the window. *The lights in the window.* "Boyd!" I shouted. "Look!"

But Boyd didn't answer, and as I turned around I saw why. Just a few yards in front of us was the blue canoe. Boyd was trembling at the sight of his comic book hero, but I only had eyes for Sophie, huddled in the middle of the canoe with her eyes all round and solemn. In the moonlight her face looked pale and thin.

"Sophie—" I shouted. And then to Boyd, "Can you turn it off?"

Boyd cut the engine and for the first time in what seemed like a very long time, it was quiet. Our little boat, only a few yards from the canoe, was now floating and bobbing with the waves.

"Sophie—" I started again, trying for a calm I didn't feel. "Are you okay?"

Sophie nodded. "We've been waiting for you. He's our uncle."

Behind me, I heard Boyd's surprised gasp. I looked past Sophie to Ratt. Even though he kept his face in shadows, he couldn't hide his glittery eyes that darted nervously from me to the shore and back again. Then I heard that strange, high-pitched voice make its angry accusation. "They're in my house," he said, his eyes staring straight into my own. "You've brought them into my house."

CHAPTER 51

WHEN I THINK ABOUT what happened next, I think about the lights on the water. It was like the brightest stars had fallen from the sky and were inching their way toward us.

"Rescue boats," Boyd whispered.

I turned to him and whispered back, "Can you get closer?"

"I'll try," he said, starting up the motor and twisting the throttle. The boat lurched forward.

"Easy," I said. "Don't scare him."

With the searchlights all around, Ratt was finding it more and more difficult to stay in the shadows. He twitched one way and then ducked the other. He seemed to have forgotten that Sophie was in the canoe. I took a deep breath to keep my voice soft and steady. "Ratt, listen," I said, "I just want Sophie. Just let us have Sophie. Then we'll leave you alone."

At first it seemed as though he hadn't heard me. Then, when he managed to find another patch of darkness to hide behind, he answered in his strange, high-pitched voice. "It's too late. Look at what you've done."

I didn't need to look. I knew what he meant. Even if Ratt managed to escape the rescue boats, the lights in the mansion would never go away. His tools and paint and mountains of trash—it could never be his hiding place again.

"It's not too late," I lied. "Everyone is just looking for Sophie. So we'll take her and you can disappear again. It will be just like before."

This time instead of answering, Ratt picked up the paddle and started to row. When Sophie realized what was happening, she jumped to her feet. "Margaret!" she cried, ready to leap across the water to me.

"Sit down!" Ratt and I both shouted it at the same time. Sophie froze, but she didn't sit down. I know my little sister—she was about to jump.

"Sit down, Sophie!" I shouted again. I turned back to Ratt. His paddle was now hovering uncertainly over the water. "Listen, she can't swim. Did you know that? My mother never lets her get close to the water. Do you want her to drown, too? Just like my dad?"

I saw Ratt's hands tighten around the paddle. He looked at me—straight up at me, and even though his face was in the shadows, those glowing eyes burned a message into mine. And if there was any doubt to what that message was, his next move made it perfectly clear: He held up the paddle and stabbed it in the water.

Swoosh.

The paddle sliced through the water like a steel blade, putting at least twenty yards of water between us in just seconds.

"Boyd, you have to get closer." I couldn't take my eyes off Sophie, who was still standing near the edge of the canoe. Little Sophie, my fearless sister.

Boyd looked down and grabbed the throttle—and that's when it happened. Our motorboat lurched forward way too fast. In an instant, we were on top of the small canoe.

"Boyd!" I screamed as he cut the engine—but it was already too late. Over the painful screech of metal on wood I heard three things I will never forget.

The first was Sophie's scream.

The second was the loud splash of a body hitting water.

The third was silence which, until that very moment, I hadn't realized was even a sound.

Silence.

I didn't stop to think about the night, the ice-cold water, the rescue boats closing in on us, anything. I didn't kick off my shoes or take off my jacket or even look to see where I was going. I just dove.

That moment in the air was long and still and almost peaceful. I remember watching the water with an outsider's interest—like I couldn't quite believe that what was happening was really, truly happening.

But it was. And what came next was cold that stung like a slap. My heart, my breath, even the blood in my veins all seemed to stop. *This is it*, I heard myself tell myself. *This is it.*

The cold froze my brain, too. For a moment I forgot to move. Then some little neuron finally remembered to do its job. "Kick," it said. "Swim."

I kicked against the weight of my waterlogged shoes and jeans, struggling to get to the surface. But, wait—was I going the right way? How could I tell? What if I'd gotten turned around? How could I tell I wasn't swimming straight down to the ocean floor? The more I thought about it, the more turned around I became; the more I fought against the weight of my clothes, the heavier they grew.

Where was the moon now? Where was the moon to guide me in the right direction? I opened my eyes. Yes, there was a glowing light above me—but there was also one below. Was one the moon and one a reflection of the moon? Or maybe both were the glowing eyes of the Drowning Ghost, coming for me after all?

This entire life, the life of me drowning, took place in just seconds. While a part of me was still frantically kicking this way and that, another part had slowed down and was watching it all through fuzzy eyes, too numb to think, too numb to feel, too numb to move. *Was this what it was like, Dad? Is this how you feel every day, Mom?*

My lungs weren't numb, though. They pounded on the inside of my chest and screamed for air. And this is where the big, hairy hand of Fate once again reached into my life. Just when my entire body was about to burst apart, I found myself being yanked up by the shoulders. Yanked, yanked and then, *AHHHHHHHH.* Air. Sky. Moon.

Air.

I coughed, sputtered, and cried, all at the same time. Choked up salt water and then swallowed some more as wave after salty wave splashed up and over my head.

"Hold on," that strange voice whispered next to me. "Hold on to my neck."

"Where's Sophie?" I tried to say, but all that came out was a mouthful of water and, "Soph—"

"She's safe. Hold on to my neck."

My teeth were chattering and I couldn't stop them; my arms and legs were as dead and heavy as planks of wood. *How very strange,* I thought. *My father drowning. The same water. The same person.* I tried to hold on to his neck, but another wave splashed up and over my head—and then another. That's when I felt my arms take on a life of their own. My body, see, thought it was dying. And so it stopped listening to my mind. My arms reached up and grabbed whatever they could find. And what they found was Ratt's head. Ratt's head was solid and above water—two things my body knew it needed for survival. I felt myself reach for his head. I felt myself pushing him under, climbing on top.

CHAPTER 52

FROM THE MOMENT HE crashed into the canoe, Boyd stood helplessly and watched as the whole world seemed to capsize. First he saw Sophie tumble head-first into the dark, choppy waves; then he watched Margaret dive in after her. He'd waited for two heads to bob up, and when they didn't, he realized that he might never be able to move again—that his own life was somehow connected to those two missing ones.

It was a loud slap against the side of the motor-boat that freed his body from its frozen spell. Boyd looked down just as Sophie's small head was being pushed up from the water. "Grab her," he heard a voice say. That same, funny voice.

As Boyd leaned over the side of the boat and grabbed hold of Sophie's arm, he found himself face-to-face with his strange, reclusive, comic book hero. Boyd was so stunned, he forgot what he was supposed to do.

"Pull!" Ratt sputtered, and Boyd pulled with all his might, bringing Sophie into the boat like a long, slip-pery fish. But as soon as Boyd turned back to the water, his hero was gone.

Boyd scanned the horizon. The lights from the rescue boats didn't seem to be getting any closer. He looked into the dark water for any sign of Margaret or

Ratt—or the Drowning Ghost. "Margaret!" he shouted. "Margaret!"

"Where's my sister?" Sophie was still crumpled on the bottom of the boat, dazed and shivering.

Boyd looked across the water one more time, then turned and crouched down next to Sophie. "He'll save her," he said. "Just like he saved you." Then he scrambled to the back of the boat and quickly grabbed two things: a wool blanket and a life preserver. The wool blanket he wrapped tightly around the shivering little body. The life preserver he clutched to his chest, ready.

It was Sophie who spotted them first—two heads bobbing up and down several yards from the capsized canoe. "I see them!" she cried. "Over there."

Boyd aimed the life preserver, then stopped.

"Why don't you throw it?" Sophie wailed.

Boyd moved to the front of the boat. "We're too far away. We need to get closer." He turned the key in the ignition. "Hang on," he shouted over his shoulder. To himself he whispered, "Hang on, Margaret." This time he would do it right.

CHAPTER 53

WHAT HAPPENED NEXT? I can't say I know exactly. My head would be above water, then under it, all the while fighting against a slow, steady tug from somewhere below. "Drowning Ghost," my groggy mind was thinking, but later I would feel the weight of my soaked jeans and tennis shoes and know otherwise.

I do know this—Ratt became my island, the one thing I clung to for life. Somehow he kept me up until Boyd came through with the life preserver.

"Here," he squeaked, placing my arms around the orange floating donut. "Hold on and don't let go."

My jaws were clenched so tightly that I couldn't speak, and my arms and legs had gone almost completely numb. But somehow I managed to hang on.

I remember noticing how close the circle of flashing bright lights had become. It was like we were suddenly onstage and under a hot spotlight. I turned to my uncle on the other side of the life preserver. For the first time ever, I saw him up close and in the light.

How can I describe what I saw? You know how there's the Superman in the comics, all red and blue and strong and bulging? Then there's the cheap, drugstore Halloween costume with unraveling seams and a cape that doesn't quite cover the shoulder blades? Instead of the fierce half man, half rodent from the books, I was looking at the sad, shabby, drugstore imitation. Dazed and scared, he was staring into the bright lights of the oncoming rescue boats. And he was exhausted. Being my island had taken just about every bit of strength he had. Why was he doing this? Why was he helping me?

The lights were practically blinding now, and the engine noise was loud in my ears. In minutes, maybe even seconds, I'd be yanked back into the real world and before that happened, I had to know. "Why are you doing this?" I yelled over the sound of the approaching engines. "Why did you bring my sister out here?"

At first I didn't think he'd heard me. Then he lowered his head so I couldn't see his face. "I wasn't going to hurt her," he said. "I just wanted to show her where it happened. I wanted to tell her the story."

"But why didn't you just tell me? Don't you know? That's why I came here."

"I know why you came here."

"My dad—" I started. "Out here—"

"And then the lights, and they are coming for me—" His head started to slip down into the water.

"No," I shouted. "Listen! Tell me. Tell me what happened."

"Nowhere left for wildlife—"

"Please. Please. I need to know—"

"Nowhere left for wildlife—"

"That night. With my dad—your brother—"

At the mention of his brother, Ratt's head snapped back up and he peered at me over the top of the life preserver, almost like he was seeing me for the first time. Then his eyes softened. "You look like him," he said. "I tried to draw him as best as I could, so that everyone would remember how wonderful he was. But that's not how he comes out. He comes out different. I keep trying. I keep trying to draw him the right way. But he won't let me. He comes out and wants revenge. He comes out and wants his life back."

"Maybe he'll go away if you tell me." I was crying now. Choking on salt water and numb to my neck. "Please," I said, "just tell me one thing." I felt myself slipping under.

"Hold on," he whispered.

"Did he want to come back to us?"

"Hold on," he said again. "Please remember that I never meant for anything bad to happen. Please believe that I'm sorry for everything. It was my fault. Of course he wanted to go back to you. Please, Margaret. You must hold on."

And then the other side of the life preserver popped up out of the water. And then I was alone.

"Ratt!" I screamed when I realized that he had let go. "Uncle Ratt!" I scanned the water for any sign of him, but there was none.

It was a rescue boat that scooped me up, stripped me out of my clothes and bundled me in layers of wool blankets. Things happened quickly after that. The police boats, the sirens, the searchlights and the questions. "My sister—" I tried to ask.

The rescue-boat man pointed over to Boyd's boat just a few yards away. "She's fine," he said. "And your friend is, too. We'll take you—"

I stopped him before he could finish. "My uncle," I said, forcing my mouth open and shut. The words moved stiffly from my numb lips. "He's still in the water."

The rescue-boat man grabbed a hand radio and mumbled a few urgent words. Immediately, the rescue boats blinked to life again, sounding sirens and flooding the waters with blinding light. I watched divers in shiny black wetsuits slide into the dark water.

"Check the canoe!" I heard someone shout and I stood holding my breath while two of the divers swam over to it. *Please, please, please,* I whispered. *Please be holding on, please.* But even before I saw the divers move away from the canoe, I knew. I already knew.

The rescue boat carrying Sophie and Boyd pulled up next to mine. "Margaret!" Sophie shouted, standing up like she was ready to leap out of the boat again. She was wrapped in blankets, just like me, but she was grinning like only Sophie could grin at a time like that.

"Can she come in here with me?" I asked the rescue man and he nodded, straddled the two boats with his long, rescue-man legs and swung her over. Then he held out a hand to Boyd, who took it and leaped across. While Sophie clung to my waist, Boyd and I looked at each other over the top of her head. *He's my uncle, he saved my life.* But I couldn't get the words out.

As if he'd heard them anyway, Boyd nodded and glanced out over the water. "He'll be fine," he said. "He's the Ratt." But his voice was shaking.

I swallowed hard and forced myself to say it. "He's my uncle," I said. *My uncle.* He had said my name like he knew me. He had told me he was sorry and that my father hadn't wanted to die. And when I'd looked into his sad, tired eyes, I knew it was the truth.

Boyd continued to watch the water. If he could still believe in the Ratt from the books, he could believe that he was out there right now, either battling the Drowning Ghost or making the greatest escape of all time.

It took a moment, but Sophie finally realized what was happening. Still clinging to my waist she called out over the water, "Uncle Ratt! Uncle Ratt!"

The rescue man spoke up gently. "Listen," he said, "we're going to take you kids in. The other boats will stay and look for your uncle."

"He was just here," I said. "He saved my life. You have to find him."

"If he's out here, they'll find him. I promise."

"I don't want to leave him, Margaret. I don't want to leave," Sophie sobbed.

"I know," I said. "It's okay, Sophie. They'll find him."

"But he just wanted to show me where it happened. He just wanted to tell me the story. He told me everything, Margaret."

"*Shhh,*" I said, pulling her into my lap. I wasn't listening to her at all. I was thinking about that one moment when I knew how easy it would have been to let myself go. Down into the dark, quiet water. Is that what Ratt had done?

As Sophie, Boyd, and I huddled together in the back, our rescue boat pulled away from the others and headed for shore. I watched the circle of searchlights blur together until they became just one spot in a huge, dark blanket of sea. That one spot had completely changed my life, not once now, but twice.

"Mom!" The minute the rescue man set Sophie on shore, she raced up the beach to Lizzie, who had already been radioed that we were okay and on our way. Lizzie dropped to her knees and held out her arms. Sophie dove into them and the two rocked together back and forth, laughing and crying, both at the same time.

"Boyd!" In the midst of the small crowd of onlookers, Boyd's mom and dad called out to their son. As Boyd ran up to them, they closed around him like two halves of an oyster shell protecting its precious pearl.

I slowly made my way to Sophie and Lizzie, still clinging to each other like those photographs of people who have just returned from war. "Come here, honey," Lizzie called to me, holding out an arm.

I walked past her, dazed still. "I have to find something first," I mumbled.

"Margaret!" I heard her call out after me and I started to run. Blanket flapping around my bare legs, I was running to the mansion, thinking that maybe Ratt had already made it to shore. Maybe the search boat was wasting its time—maybe Ratt was back in his little room, hunched over his desk, sketching out an adventure about three kids who follow him out on the water. That's what I was running for and hoping to find: Ratt turning this terrible night into a thrilling story that we could all hang on to and read over and over and over again.

I walked around the side of the house. On the porch was a police officer, guarding the front door. I stood in the shadows, watching. What could I do now?

Boyd ran up to me then, flustered and out of breath. "Margaret, there you are. I got so scared. Your mom is looking for you. You're all staying at our place tonight." Numbly, I let Boyd take my arm and lead me back to his house. He nodded his head toward the lights on the water. "They're still out there," he said. "It means there's hope, right?"

I didn't know how to answer him. I'd seen Ratt up close. I'd looked into his very human eyes and heard him say, "It's too late now," and, "Nowhere left for wildlife." I'd seen his trembling hands slip from the life preserver, taking his story with him.

CHAPTER 54

WHEN WE REACHED THE house, Boyd's mom gave me a hug like she'd known me for years. Sophie was tucked in and snoring on the sofa, and my mom was sitting at the kitchen table, drinking herbal tea. If you ever want instant best friends, throw yourself in a crisis.

"Can I get you something to eat?" Boyd's mom asked me. "Something hot to drink?"

I shook my head. Lizzie cleared her throat nervously and motioned to the chair next to hers.

"How did you know we were here?" I asked her.

"I got a phone call."

Boyd's mom said, "We put a sleeping bag in the living room for you. Boyd can get you some clothes."

"Thanks," I said.

"Go on," Boyd's mom said to Lizzie. To me she said, "Your mother was explaining your connection to the house next door." She shook her head. "Remarkable story."

"Right," I said. "Don't stop on my account. I've been waiting to hear it for a long time."

Lizzie cleared her throat. "Margaret, I was just saying that after your grandfather died, your uncle was out here all alone and was, well, getting a little crazy."

Boyd's mother poured her another cup of herbal

tea. "I had no idea anyone was living there. And he actually thought he was a rat? He went through people's garbage?" She shook her head and shuddered.

"It started when he was young," Lizzie explained. "Puberty." The two mothers glanced at me and Boyd, then back to each other.

I couldn't sit still and listen any longer. "He sent you a package, Mom. He tried to contact you. You didn't even open it!"

"I couldn't open it, Margaret. I couldn't."

"Why?"

But my mother didn't answer. Her hand twitched like it was looking for its cigarette. Just then, Boyd's dad walked through the front door. He'd been out at the beach, watching the search boats.

"Dad!" Boyd ran up to him, waiting for news.

His father glanced at his mother, then at Lizzie, then at me. He put his hands on Boyd's shoulders. "They're calling it off for tonight," he said. "They'll start again in the morning."

Calling it off for tonight. Like it was a rained-out baseball game.

Without a word, Boyd and I turned and walked down the hallway to his room. In the closet I quickly slipped into a sweatshirt and a pair of his jeans, then together we stood at his bedroom window and looked out over the water. The bright lights of the rescue boats were coming in, splitting off in different directions like giant fireworks exploding in slow motion. If it wasn't so chest-hurting sad, it might have been something beautiful to watch.

I heard Boyd's door open and a moment later Lizzie stood behind us. I could tell it was her by the stale cigarette smell on her clothes. "Margaret," she said quietly, "I couldn't open it. Opening it would have made me live through it all over again, and I barely made it through the first time."

The three of us stood in silence, watching the searchlights moving closer to shore. "Mom," I said softly, "Dad wanted to come back to us. Ratt told me out there."

"Of course he did, honey."

"You knew?"

"It was an accident, Margaret. You knew that—"

"No I didn't, Mom. You never talked about it. You never talked about anything. And then you started sleeping all the time. I thought it was because—I thought Dad—" I couldn't finish.

"Boyd, would you mind giving us a minute—"

"No," I said quickly. "It's his room. If you have something to say, I want Boyd to hear it, too."

Lizzie hesitated for a moment, then sighed. "Okay," she said. "Margaret, honey. Your sister told me something tonight, right before she fell asleep. When your uncle took her out in the canoe, he wanted to show her where it had happened—"

"I already know this, Mom."

Lizzie continued like I hadn't said a word. "He was

also using her as bait—his words, not hers. He wanted to show you the place, too, and he knew you'd follow them out there. He told her something, Margaret. He told her everything that happened that night. And there's more to the story than I knew."

I watched the searchlights moving closer to shore. Why had he told Sophie and not me? I thought about my little sister, marching up to the mansion and encountering Ratt for the first time. Her sweet little face in the comic he drew. *We have a white rat named Glenda in a cage in my school. We feed her sunflower seeds.* That's why.

"Margaret, your father had come here to bring Ratt back to live with us. We'd visited him, especially after your grandfather's death, but when people started filing complaints about him going through their garbage, that's when we knew he couldn't live here alone anymore."

Only half of me was listening. The other half was playing the Happy-Ending Game—watching the water, waiting for a large rodent head to pop up and bounce merrily toward shore.

I heard Lizzie take a shaky breath. "Well, Ratt knew your father was coming and that he'd just keep coming. He told your father that if he left this place, he didn't think he'd be able to survive—"

"No place left for wildlife," I said.

"What?" Boyd asked.

"It's what he said to me out there. He said there

was no place left for wildlife."

"Go on," Boyd said, turning to my mom. "What was it he told Sophie?"

Maybe it was Boyd's prompting that made her launch into the rest. Like it was burning her throat to hold it in any longer, the story suddenly spilled from her mouth. And as she spoke, I started to hear his voice. The sad, raspy voice of my uncle, the Ratt. This is what he'd told Sophie, out on the canoe. This is his story.

To disappear completely and never be found, you must have a witness, he said.

Ratt's witness was my father.

I would take him out in the canoe one last time, just like when we were kids. I'd go out far and tell him I wanted one last swim. He would watch from the canoe as I drifted farther and farther away. "Be careful," he would yell, just like when we were kids. And that's when I'd do it. It would be difficult—I didn't want to cause him pain. But it was the only way for me. I had to pretend to drown and I had to have a witness. My brother would mourn me for a while, then he'd go back to his life with his wife and his daughters. And I could go on being the Ratt.

I knew he was an excellent swimmer, so I wasn't worried about him—all I worried about was getting away and making my escape.

Except that's not how it went. My dad went in after him. The canoe drifted. The water was icy cold. They struggled in the water. Ratt swam away. He heard my father calling for him, but he didn't realize that he was actually calling for help. My dad was a champion swimmer. He had always been Ratt's hero. How could Ratt know that it was real, my dad's call for help?

That it was real.

This was what I'd come to the island to find. And when the story was finished, the whole world looked different. I'd met my father out there in the water. I'd felt him both pull me under and then push me up. I'd seen the reflection of him in my uncle's eyes, the moment my uncle had looked into my own. That was it. My HARDEST JIGSAW was complete.

I opened my eyes to my reflection in the glass. "So he drew him," I said softly, watching my lips move but hearing my voice like it was coming from somewhere else. "That's how he tried to keep him alive. But he didn't come out right. He came out like a ghost. Boyd, I guess you know. My dad is the Drowning Ghost."

"Yes," said Boyd. His voice squeaked when he said it.

"And the package, Mom. He wanted to say he was sorry. He needed to tell you what had happened. He gave you a key to the house." I waited for her to say something, but she didn't. "You sent it back. You didn't even open it. So he lived alone with this terrible story inside him, all these years. And now he's dead because of me. He saved my life and now he's gone." I hadn't even known I was crying until I looked down at the windowsill wet with tears. I thought about my uncle as a boy, truly believing he was turning into a hideous creature. I thought about him years later, full of pain and guilt. We were more related than he would ever know.

"Maybe he's still out there," Boyd said. "Maybe he's still alive."

"No," Lizzie said firmly. "The water's too cold. He's gone. And he's at peace. Finally—he's at peace."

I felt Boyd's shoulder tremble against mine. I buried my face in my hands. Maybe he was at peace, but what about me? "This is all your fault," I said to my mother. "Your fault." I didn't mean it, really. I knew there was a lot I would never understand—like what it must have been like to have two small kids and a dead husband. But I wanted to hurt someone as much as I hurt. And I wanted it to be her.

Lizzie was quiet for a moment, then she said, "I'm sorry. I'm sorry, Margaret." I felt her move away from me and, through the reflection in the window, I watched her leave the room.

Boyd slid open the window. Without speaking, we climbed over the ledge and ran down to the beach, straight to Ratt's dock. We walked to the very end and sat down, close enough so that our shoulders were touching again. I leaned forward and dipped my hands in the water. "This is the same water," I whispered, "the same water." I didn't say it out loud but I knew Boyd knew. *The same water where my father still is. My father the Drowning Ghost.*

"I lied about him," Boyd blurted out suddenly.

"What?"

"It was the Threes that tied me up. Ratt just made the comic so you would find me."

"Oh," I said. "Oh." *Of course.*

Boyd looked down at his own hands and started to cry.

We spent the night out there on the dock, both of us waiting for the Ratt to drag himself to shore, shake his furry body and scurry to the safety of his mansion. But as we watched the sun push the moon out of the sky, we knew. We didn't say it out loud, but we both knew.

CHAPTER 55

AS PROMISED THE RESCUE boats were out on the water first thing the next morning. But, as Boyd's dad was quick to point out over breakfast, "They're not looking for a survivor, son."

"What does that mean?" asked Sophie, sniffing her tofu-bacon strips suspiciously.

"It means they're still looking for him, honey," said Lizzie.

"Tell her the truth, Mom," I said. After everything that had happened, wasn't it the one thing we could take back with us?

Lizzie looked down at her plate. She cleared her throat. "It means," she said slowly, "that he probably isn't alive." She looked up and touched Sophie's hand. "I'm sorry, honey." But even before the words were out, Sophie knew. She was already crying.

I avoided the beach the rest of the morning and didn't even glance at the two boats still circling the waters. Instead, I went into the house to get my backpack, the comic book, and Ratt's dog.

I found my backpack, exactly where I'd left it, but the police must have taken the comic as evidence. The dog was either hiding and wouldn't be fooled by the tofu bacon I was using as bait, or maybe he, too, was simply gone.

I slung my backpack over my shoulder, then took one last look around the run-down old mansion. *Good-bye, Dad.*

As I stepped out into the sunshine, I thought, *How can this sun feel good on my face?* I looked across the lawn at Lizzie, just finishing up with the police officer. The officer nodded, closed his notebook and tucked his pen in his pocket. I wondered what they would do with all the notes he'd taken—if maybe a small article would appear in the weekly paper and if maybe Mr. Librarian would find it, clip it, and add it to one of his scrapbooks. And if he did, which scrapbook would it be? HUMAN INTEREST? AMAZING ANIMAL STORIES? THINGS THAT HAPPENED LONG AGO BUT STILL HAUNT US TODAY?

Boyd stood in the middle of the lawn, staring at the For Sale sign that Lizzie had discovered behind a bush and stuck back in the ground. I stepped off the porch and made my way over to him. This was going to be it. This was going to be good-bye.

"I'm sorry about the sign," I said.

"I'll take it down when you leave," he said. That was all he said, but I knew what he was thinking. *Just in case.*

"Boyd," I started, then stopped. Everything I wanted to say got stuck in my mouth, so instead I said, "I tried to get *Volume 1* for you, but the police must have taken it."

"That's okay."

We stared at each other, waiting for the moment that would have to come next, that saying good-bye moment that neither one of us wanted. There was so much I wanted to say. *Thank you for helping me find my uncle, thank you for letting me sleep underneath your bed. Thank you for sneaking me food, thank you for following me into the woods. Thank you for taking me out in the boat, even though you thought you were going to die. Thank you for sitting close enough to let me feel your shoulder tremble.* "See you," was all I said.

"'Bye, Margaret," was all he said back.

Just then Sophie burst out of the house, lugging her suitcase down the steps. "Help her with that, Margaret," Lizzie called from the truck. Now that the police business was done, she was jumpy to get going. "Hurry. I want to catch the next ferry."

I grabbed Sophie's suitcase and walked across the yard, glad to have something to do.

"Be careful, my puzzle," Sophie said, skipping ahead and hopping into the truck.

"What does she have in there?" Boyd asked.

"A jigsaw," I said, setting the suitcase in the back of the truck. Then I turned back to Boyd and we smiled. We looked at each other, straight at each other, and smiled. In the sunlight, the night before didn't seem quite real. In the sunlight, Boyd's eyes were the color of deep, clear water.

Sophie honked the horn. I walked to the door and climbed inside.

"You know where I live," Boyd called out as Lizzie put the truck in reverse and pulled out of the driveway. I nodded and waved to him through the open window.

The crunch of wheels on the gravel drive, the smell of grass in the sun, the sound of crickets calling out hello and good-bye. *Remember this*, I said to myself. Remember every bit of this. Remember a boy who looked at himself in the mirror and believed he saw a hideous thing. Remember a boy who treasured things that other people threw away. Remember a boy who learned to survive. Remember a boy who became my uncle and saved my life—the terrible, wonderful Ratt.

Just then I heard the sound of a dog barking. Sophie turned around in her seat. "Mom, stop!" she cried. I looked, too. Ratt's dog was running next to the truck, trying to sink his long teeth into our moving tire.

"Mom, stop," I said. "We need to get him."

Lizzie glanced in her rearview mirror, but didn't slow down. "He'll be all right," she said. "Boyd will feed him."

"Was that a Chihuahua, Margaret?" Sophie asked after the dog was out of sight. I didn't answer.

We drove through town to get to the ferry terminal. *Good-bye, Drugstore*, I said to myself. *Good-bye, cherry-filled donuts and old man eating a hamburger. Good-bye, Mr. Librarian and all your scrapbooks. Good-bye, B for Boyd and R for Ratt.*

Lizzie gave us money for food on the ferry and when

Sophie came back with a giant plate of fries, Lizzie asked me, "Don't you want something, Margaret?" I shook my head and continued to stare out the window.

"Tina Louise has a boyfriend," said Sophie, seven fries hanging out of her mouth.

I ignored her.

"She has a boyfriend and she says it was Fate that brought them together. I saw them before I came to get you."

I ignored her.

"Margaret, what's Fate?"

I got up and stomped past her. I stepped onto the deck and found a place at the railing. Sophie followed me out. "You want a french fry for the seagulls?" she asked.

"Leave me alone, Sophie."

"Just tell me what's Fate."

I turned to her in disbelief. How could she be acting so happy? How could she be eating french fries? "Do you even know what happened last night?" I asked her. "Do you even remember what happened?"

Sophie reached into her shirt and pulled out the swimming medal I'd given her the night before I left for the island.

"I mean it, Sophie," I said. "Leave me alone."

"No, don't you get it?" she said. "This was in my suitcase today. I got it right before we left. My suitcase in the *mansion*."

I stared at her, trying to understand what she was trying to tell me. "So what?" I said.

"I gave it to him last night. When we were in the canoe."

"What?" I noticed that my heart was beating and wondered if maybe it had been frozen since the night before.

"He put it around his neck," she said.

I ran back inside and grabbed my backpack from the seat next to Lizzie. I unzipped the top and felt around. Clothes, candy bars, flashlight, wait. My hand closed around the spine of a book. I took a deep breath and pulled it out. *Ratt Volume 1: How to Disappear Completely and Never Be Found.*

"What's that, Margaret?" Lizzie asked.

"It's a book," I said slowly. "It's his book." I leafed through the pages. Tucked carefully in the middle was the newspaper article from the library: LOCAL BOY HEADING FOR GOLD. I glanced out the window at Sophie, still on the deck. "Mom, this book was in the house—" Then I stopped. Sophie was jumping up and down and waving her arms at something on the water. She turned back, looked at me through the window, and motioned for me to *hurry!* I clutched the book to my chest and ran back to the deck.

"Sophie, what is it?" But before she could answer, I saw what it was. Weaving through sleek little sailboats and gleaming yachts, a small motorboat raced toward our ferry.

"It's them, Margaret!" Sophie shouted gleefully. "It's them!"

Boyd, the boy once terrified of being on water,

was driving the boat like he'd been doing it all his life. "Boyd!" I waved my arms in the air, just like Sophie. He couldn't have heard me over the roar of the engines, but still, something made him look up. He saw us and waved back, then turned to the lone figure huddled in the back of the boat.

And that's when it happened.

My uncle, the Ratt, stood up. For the first time in years, he stood up in the light of day and let the sun shine on his face. Shyly, he raised his arm to me, and then to Sophie.

"Uncle Raaaaattttt!" we screamed, laughing and crying and hugging each other. "Uncle Raaaaattttt!" until our throats stung and our voices were hoarse.

I don't know how long she'd been standing there, but suddenly I noticed Lizzie's hands gripping the railing next to me. "Mom," I whispered, but she didn't seem to hear. She let go of the railing and reached out her hand. Ratt, from the back of the motorboat, reached his out, too. And even with all that space and water between them, I could tell their hands were touching.

"Mom," I said, but I didn't know what to say after that. I just wanted to say the word. "Mom," I said again, and this time I was crying too hard to say anything else. She put her arm around me, then reached over and grabbed Sophie. The three of us stood there, all together like that, while Boyd turned the boat in a large circle and headed back to the island.

CHAPTER 56

HE CAME BACK. He'd pulled off the greatest escape of all time and could have easily disappeared forever, like he'd been trying to do for years. But he came back. I think he didn't want me to be trapped by the same guilt he'd been living with since my dad died. I think that's why.

At first I thought this story ended with that wave on the ferry. But just like I'm not sure where it really began, I'm not so sure about the ending, either.

A week after we returned from the island, Lizzie had a long meeting with some people at the bank. Apparently, years ago, my grandfather (who died when I was too young to remember him) had set up a fund for his youngest son. This fund would take care of all the house expenses so that, once my grandfather was gone, Ratt would never have to worry about a thing—all the property taxes on the mansion and land would be automatically paid each year. That way my father, too, would never have to be burdened with his strange, reclusive brother. But then the fund ran out and when the bank people couldn't find any trace of Ratt, the house had become Lizzie's property and responsibility.

"That's why the For Sale by Owner sign," whispered Sophie. We were sitting on the couch in the bankers' office, trying to make sense of all the grown-up money talk that was buzzing around our heads.

"I guess so," I whispered back, waiting for the next bit of business that I would only half understand. Instead, I saw my mother grab her checkbook and scribble out a check. Handing it to the bank people, she told them to contact her with all future house expenses and legal matters.

"Does that mean we're moving there, Mom?" Sophie piped up hopefully from the back of the room. Even though I kept my mouth shut, I was hopeful, too.

"No," she answered without turning around. "We're not selling it, that's all." And the way she said it made us know not to ask anything else.

A few days later, a large manila envelope addressed to Elizabeth Clairmont arrived in the mail. I recognized the handwriting right away. Mom opened the envelope slowly and took out a drawing. It was a drawing of the mansion the way it might have looked many years before—a beautiful place someone would be proud to live. Underneath the drawing were two words. *Thank you.*

We all stared at it for a long time. Then without a word, Mom went to the kitchen and stuck it on the refrigerator with the pink hippo refrigerator magnet. "Maybe we'll go there once in a while," she said, still staring at the drawing. "Maybe we can fix some of those broken windows one of these weekends. Do something with that yard." Sophie and I just looked at each other and grinned.

Every couple of weeks Boyd would bundle up the latest Ratt books and send them to me. I'd read them right away, then later that night, read them aloud to Sophie in bed. I usually held on to them for a few days, then went to the post office and mailed them back to Boyd, even though he said that I should keep them since Ratt was my uncle and all. But I knew they belonged with Boyd. He was the one who had discovered them and treasured them, long before they were as popular as they are now.

The books are pretty much the same except for one thing: The Drowning Ghost no longer appears on full-moon nights, looking for revenge and a new pair of eyes. Maybe it's because, as Boyd wrote in one of his letters, all he ever really wanted was to see his children one last time. And now that he has, he can rest in peace.

When I think about it all, I realize that this isn't just my story, and where it begins and ends for me isn't where it begins and ends for anyone else. Take Tina Louise, for example. When I got back to Holy Names, an amazing thing had happened. Tina Louise had learned to play baseball. "How did this happen?" I asked, not quite believing it was true.

Tina Louise just looked at me in wonder and shook her head. "Fate," she said simply. "It was Fate." But after all I've been through, I don't feel the same about Fate anymore. Sometimes things just happen—both good and bad—and it's up to us to make sense of them when they do. It might have been Fate that got her knocked flat on her back that day, but when the baseball lessons came her way, it was Tina Louise who said yes to them.

Apparently, the same day I'd left for the island, D.J. had approached Tina Louise on the playfield and offered to teach her how to play ball. "Who are you trying to humiliate this time?" she asked him, and only when his ears turned bright pink did she realize he was being completely sincere.

Now, the thing is, not only had D.J. taught her to catch a ball, but together they discovered that Tina Louise had the most remarkable talent the world of baseball had ever seen. I saw it for myself the first day back at P.E. Tina Louise would stand in the outfield, balancing on her hands. A batter would hit the ball and, as the ball flew through the air, Tina Louise would continue to balance in a handstand; then, at the very last minute, she'd drop to her feet, hold up her glove and snag the ball from the air—like a magnet to pure metal.

It was such an amazing thing to watch that P.E. baseball became a game of target, with Tina Louise as the bull's-eye. And no matter where she placed herself in the outfield, she never missed. Even when it seemed too late and the ball looked dangerously close, Tina Louise would flip down, and in one smooth move, stick out that arm for the perfect catch.

And then everyone would cheer. The infield, the

outfield, Mrs. P.E., the opposing team. Regardless of which team they were on or how many outs there were or who was winning and by how much, everyone would stand and cheer like crazy when Tina Louise did her amazing thing. And I cheered with all the rest of them—just as happy, just as proud.

Even when she caught the first ball I ever hit.

Editor's Very Last Note:

Life changed for Boyd, too. The Threes continued to harass him for a while, but once they realized he was no longer afraid of them, they immediately gave up and began searching for their next victim.

One day, a few weeks before summer vacation, Boyd was walking down the hallway, reading the latest Ratt adventure. "Why are you always reading those?" a boy asked, staring at the strange book with the hand-drawn mansion on the cover.

Even though Boyd could feel his face turning red, he held his head high and answered, "Because they're the greatest stories ever told."

"Really?" the boy asked him.

"Really," Boyd said. And since it was lunchtime anyway, the two boys found themselves walking toward the cafeteria. As they sat down at an empty table, Boyd started from the beginning. "Once, there were two boys, much like you and me." He didn't stop until the bell rang.

"Meet me here tomorrow," said the boy. "You can tell me the rest."

The next day in the cafeteria, Boyd and the boy pooled their change and bought a plate of Tater Tots. Then, they sat down at the same table and Boyd continued the story.

The next day they met at the same table in the cafeteria, but this time they weren't alone. Two other boys, who had been sitting nearby the day before, asked shyly, "Can we listen, too?" Pretty soon, the table was packed with both boys and girls, sharing plates of Tater Tots and listening to the story of two boys, very much like them, et cetera.

"Where can we get these?" the kids asked, and when Boyd told them, there was practically a stampede to the little yellow library after school that day. Of course, there weren't enough books to go around, so Boyd started bringing in the old volumes that had been neatly stacked away in his closet. But soon even that wasn't enough to satisfy every kid who wanted to keep current with Ratt's life and adventures. Someone asked Mr. Librarian if there couldn't possibly be multiple copies of new editions, to which he replied, "Of course not."

So the kids went straight to the source. Gathering up their courage, they approached the formidable old mansion with small offerings in hand. Fear and excitement made their young hearts beat wildly as they left pieces of fruit, bags *of marbles, fistfuls of candy and, of course, boxes of cherry-filled donuts on Ratt's sagging front porch. Along with these goodies, they left letters, which usually went something like this:*

Dear Mr. Ratt,
We like your stories. It's hard to wait till they get passed around. Can you make more copies of each one?
Your Friend,
Richard or Chris or Shelley or Max

No one ever saw any sign of life coming from the house, but as if by magic, the fruit and donuts and marbles and candy would be gone. Then, the very next day, multiple copies of a new Ratt book would appear in the library under R for rodent. (Around the same time, a rumor circulated about a broken-down Xerox machine that had disappeared from the alley behind the dentist's office. But since the story never appeared in the Weekly Islander's *police beat, I still must consider it just a rumor.)*

So that's where this story will end for now. I've tried to stay out of it as much as possible, and let the people it belongs to tell it in their own words, but there are places where a third eye can be useful, don't you think?

I will say this. People leave their stories everywhere. On tiny scraps of paper and initials scratched in wooden benches. In bits of conversation overheard at a bus stop or floating out from a second-story window on a warm, summer day. In what they throw away but shouldn't, and in what they should throw away but can't. Even on grocery lists, if you squint your eyes and look at them long enough.

Everyone has a story to tell. I simply collect and preserve them. Then I try to pass them along to others who will care about them, too.

Thank You Very Sincerely
for Being One
to Pass This On To,

Mr. Librarian